«МАЛЫШ»

Григорий ОСТЕР

ВРЕДНЫЕ СОВЕТЫ

ПОСЛУШНЫМ ДЕТЯМ ЧИТАТЬ ЗАПРЕЩАЕТСЯ!

Художник

дядя Коля Воронцов

Если вы с утра решили
Хорошо себя вести,
Смело в шкаф себя ведите
И ныряйте в темноту.
Там ни мамы нет, ни папы,
Только папины штаны.
Там никто не крикнет громко:
«Прекрати! Не смей! Не тронь!»
Там гораздо проще будет,
Не мешая никому,
Целый день себя прилично
И порядочно вести.

Иноземный шпион

Е сли вы гуляли в шапке,
А потом она пропала,
Не волнуйтесь, маме дома
Можно что-нибудь соврать.
Но старайтесь врать красиво,
Чтобы, глядя восхищённо,
Затаив дыханье, мама
Долго слушала враньё.

Хенде хох!

Но уж если вы наврали
Про потерянную шапку,
Что её в бою неравном
Отобрал у вас шпион,
Постарайтесь, чтобы мама
Не ходила возмущаться
В иностранную разведку,
Там её не так поймут.

Иностранный шпион

Если вы в футбол играли
На широкой мостовой
И, ударив по воротам,
Вдруг услышали свисток,
Не кричите: «Гол!», возможно,
Это милиционер
Засвистел, когда попали
Не в ворота, а в него.

Если друг твой самый лучший
Поскользнулся и упал,
Покажи на друга пальцем
И хватайся за живот.
Пусть он видит, лежа в луже,—
Ты ничуть не огорчён.
Настоящий друг не любит
Огорчать своих друзей.

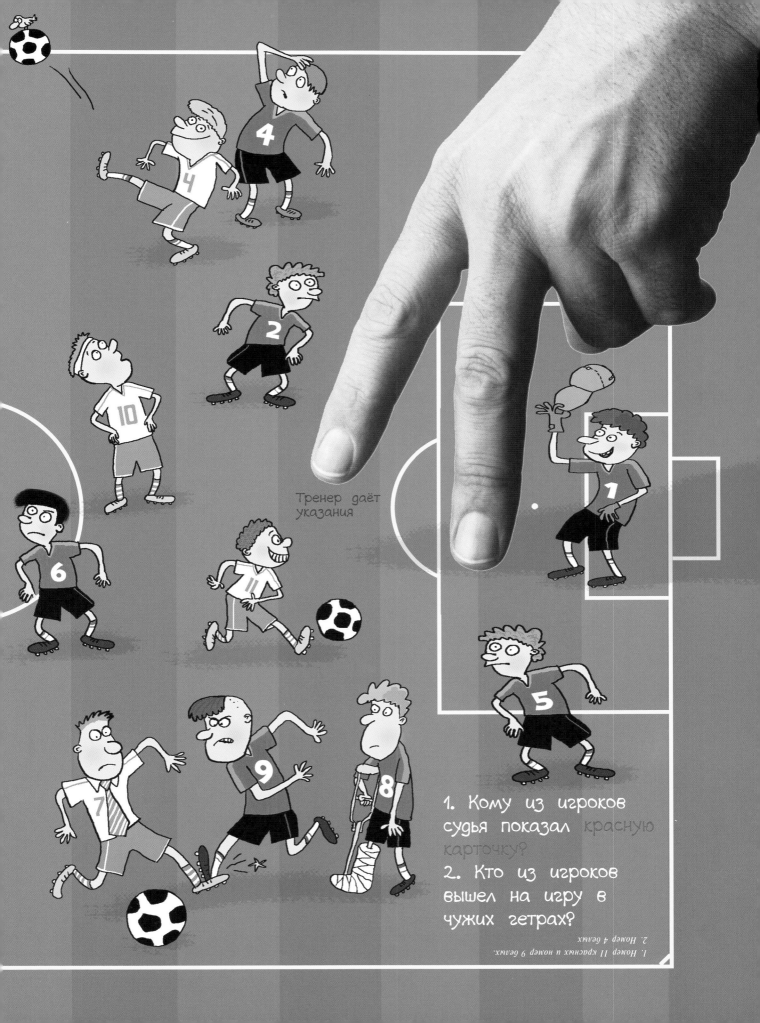

Тренер даёт указания

1. Кому из игроков судья показал красную карточку?

2. Кто из игроков вышел на игру в чужих гетрах?

1. Номер 11 красных и номер 9 белых.
2. Номер 4 белых

Убегая от трамвая,
Не спеши под самосвал.
Погоди у светофора,
Не покажется пока
«Скорой помощи» машина —
В ней полным полно врачей
Пусть они тебя задавят.
Сами вылечат потом.

Если в кухне тараканы
Маршируют по столу
И устраивают мыши
На полу учебный бой,
Значит, вам пора на время
Прекратить борьбу за мир
И все силы ваши бросить
На борьбу за чистоту.

Гений чистоты
баба Клава

Если всей семьёй купаться
Вы отправились к реке,
Не мешайте папе с мамой
Загорать на берегу.
Не устраивайте крика,
Дайте взрослым отдохнуть.
Ни к кому не приставая,
Постарайтесь утонуть.

Чтобы выгнать из квартиры
Разных мух и комаров,
Надо сдернуть занавеску
И крутить над головой.
Полетят со стен картины,
С подоконника – цветы.
Кувыркнётся телевизор,
Люстра врежется в паркет.
И, от грохота спасаясь,
Разлетятся комары,
А испуганные мухи
Стаей кинутся на юг.

Никогда не разрешайте
Ставить градусник себе,
И таблеток не глотайте,
И не ешьте порошков.
Пусть болят живот и зубы,
Горло, уши, голова,
Всё равно лекарств не пейте
И не слушайте врача.
Перестанет биться сердце,
Но зато наверняка
Не прилепят вам горчичник
И не сделают укол.

Когда состаришься — ходи

Когда состаришься — ходи
По улице пешком.
Не лезь в автобус, всё равно
Стоять придётся там.
И нынче мало дураков,
Чтоб место уступать,
А к тем далёким временам
Не станет их совсем.

Счастливый билет.
Рекомендуется съесть.

Посещайте почаще
Театральный буфет.
Там пирожные с кремом,
С пузырьками вода.
Как дрова, на тарелках
Шоколадки лежат,
И сквозь трубочку можно
Пить молочный коктейль.
Не просите билеты
На балкон и в партер,
Пусть дадут вам билеты
В театральный буфет.
Уходя из театра,
Унесёте с собой
Под трепещущим сердцем,
В животе, бутерброд.

. . . .

1. 2. 3.

Расположите картинки по порядку — до буфета, в буфете, после буфета.
. . . .

Никогда не мойте руки,
Шею, уши и лицо.
Это глупое занятье
Не приводит ни к чему.
Вновь испачкаются руки,
Шея, уши и лицо,
Так зачем же тратить силы,
Время попусту терять?
Стричься тоже бесполезно,
Никакого смысла нет:
К старости сама собою
Облысеет голова.

1×1=1	2×1=2
1×2=2	2×2=4
1×3=3	2×3=6
1×4=4	2×4=8
1×5=5	2×5=10
1×6=6	2×6=12
1×7=7	2×7=14
1×8=8	2×8=16
1×9=9	2×9=18
3×1=3	4×1=4
3×2=6	4×2=8
3×3=9	4×3=12
3×4=12	4×4=16
3×5=15	4×5=20
3×6=18	4×6=24
3×7=21	4×7=28
3×8=24	4×8=32
3×9=27	4×9=36
5×1=5	
5×2=10	
5×3=15	
5×4=20	
5×5=25	
5×6=30	
5×7=35	
5×8=40	
5×9=45	
7×1=7	8×1=8
7×2=14	8×2=16
7×3=21	8×3=24
7×4=28	8×4=32
7×5=35	8×5=40
7×6=42	8×6=48
7×7=49	8×7=56
7×8=56	8×8=64
7×9=63	8×9=72
9×1=9	
9×2=18	
9×3=27	
9×4=36	
9×5=45	
9×6=54	
9×7=63	
9×8=72	
9×9=81	

Адрес школы, той, в которой
Посчастливилось учиться,
Как таблицу умноженья,
Помни твёрдо, наизусть,
И когда тебе случится
Повстречаться с диверсантом,
Не теряя ни минуты,
Адрес школы сообщи.

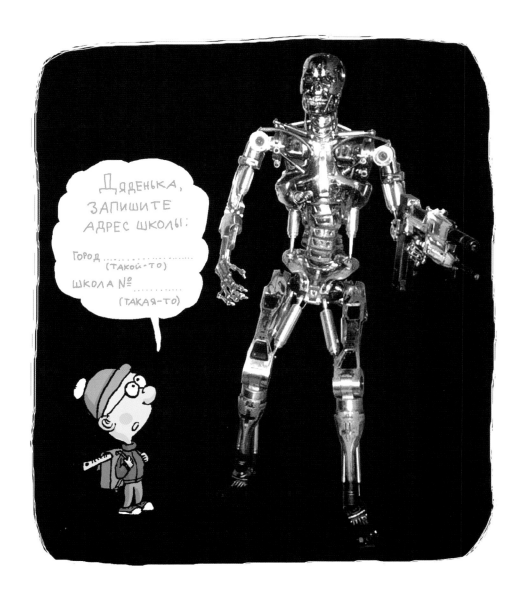

Не бери чужое, если
На тебя глядят чужие.
Пусть они глаза закроют
Или выйдут на часок.
А своих чего бояться!
Про своих свои не скажут.
Пусть глядят.
Хватай чужое
И тащи его к своим.

Чужие здесь не ходят.

30

Сейчас как
БА-А-А-ХНЕТ!

Девчонок надо никогда
Нигде не замечать.
И не давать прохода им
Нигде и никогда.
Им надо ножки подставлять,
Пугать из-за угла,
Чтоб сразу поняли они:
До них вам дела нет.
Девчонку встретил — быстро ей
Показывай язык.
Пускай не думает она,
Что ты в нее влюблён.

Задаваки!

32

Родился девочкой — терпи
Подножки и толчки.
И подставляй косички всем,
Кто дёрнуть их не прочь.
Зато когда-нибудь потом
Покажешь кукиш им
И скажешь: «Фигушки, за вас
Я замуж не пойду!»

Например, у вас в кармане
Оказалась горсть конфет,
А навстречу вам попались
Ваши верные друзья.
Не пугайтесь и не прячьтесь,
Не кидайтесь убегать,
Не пихайте все конфеты
Вместе с фантиками в рот.
Подойдите к ним спокойно,
Лишних слов не говоря,
Быстро вынув из кармана,
Протяните им… ладонь.
Крепко руки им пожмите,
Попрощайтесь не спеша
И, свернув за первый угол,
Мчитесь быстренько домой.
Чтобы дома съесть конфеты,
Залезайте под кровать,
Потому что там, конечно,
Вам не встретится никто.

Верные друзья попались навстречу.

Как принести домой конфеты
и не встретиться по пути с друзьями?

Не обижайтесь на того,
Кто бьёт руками вас,
И не ленитесь каждый раз
Его благодарить
За то, что не жалея сил,
Он вас руками бьёт,
А мог бы в эти руки взять
И палку, и кирпич.

ФЬЮИТЬ!

Надо побыстее драпать с этой страницы!

Если вас по телефону
Обозвали дураком
И не стали ждать ответа,
Бросив трубку на рычаг,
Наберите быстро номер
Из любых случайных цифр
И тому, кто снимет трубку,
Сообщите — сам дурак.

©Красная Бурда

Снимаю трубку.
Говорю: "Не туда попали!"
Кладу трубку.
Тел. 742-01-3454

Тел. 742-01-3454 | Тел. 742-01-3454 | Тел. 742-01-3454 | | Тел. 742-01-3454 | Тел. 742-01-3454 | Тел. 742-01-3454

Если вас поймала мама
За любимым делом вашим,
Например, за рисованьем
В коридоре на обоях,
Объясните ей, что это —
Ваш сюрприз к Восьмому марта.
Называется картина:
«Милой мамочки портрет».

Уголок.
Стой здесь
не шевелясь

Руками никогда нигде
Не трогай ничего.
Не впутывайся ни во что
И никуда не лезь.
В сторонку молча отойди,
Стань скромно в уголке
И тихо стой, не шевелясь,
До старости своей.

32

33

34

35

36

С мигалкой
вперёд

Пройди
техническое
обслуживание
и пропусти
ход

37

38

Возьми кубик и бросай!

39

Вперёд

40

Начинаем
игру

Начни ещё раз
сначала

Вперёд
к главному
призу

1   2   3   5   6   7   8

Нель-зяяяяя!

Как я зол!!!

Если не купили вам пирожное
И в кино с собой не взяли вечером,
Нужно на родителей обидеться
И уйти без шапки в ночь холодную.
Но не просто так
Бродить по улицам,
А в дремучий тёмный
Лес отправиться.
Там вам сразу волк
Голодный встретится
И, конечно, быстро
Вас он скушает.
Вот тогда узнают папа с мамою,
Закричат, заплачут, и забегают,
И помчатся покупать пирожное,
И в кино с собой
Возьмут вас вечером.

Ну-с,
кого тут
скушать?

Нямнямус Кровожадный

Когда тебя родная мать
Ведёт к зубным врачам,
Не жди пощады от неё,
Напрасных слёз не лей.
Молчи, как пленный партизан,
И стисни зубы так,
Чтоб не сумела их разжать
Толпа зубных врачей.

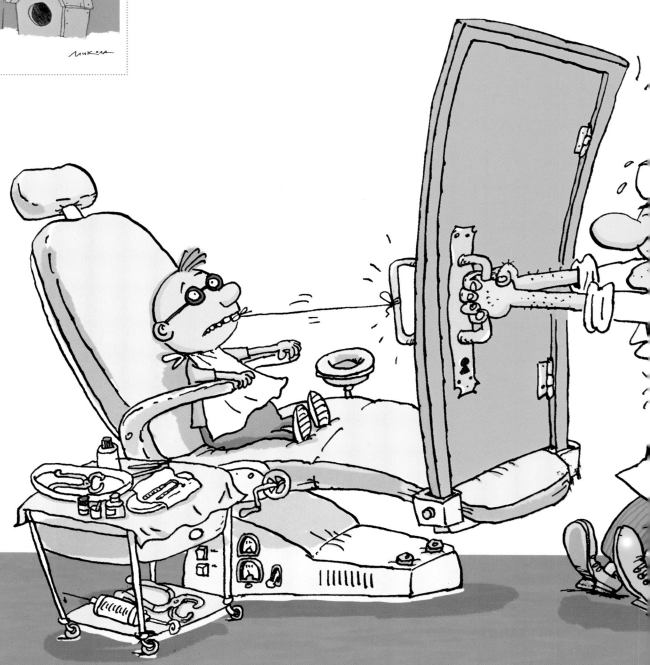

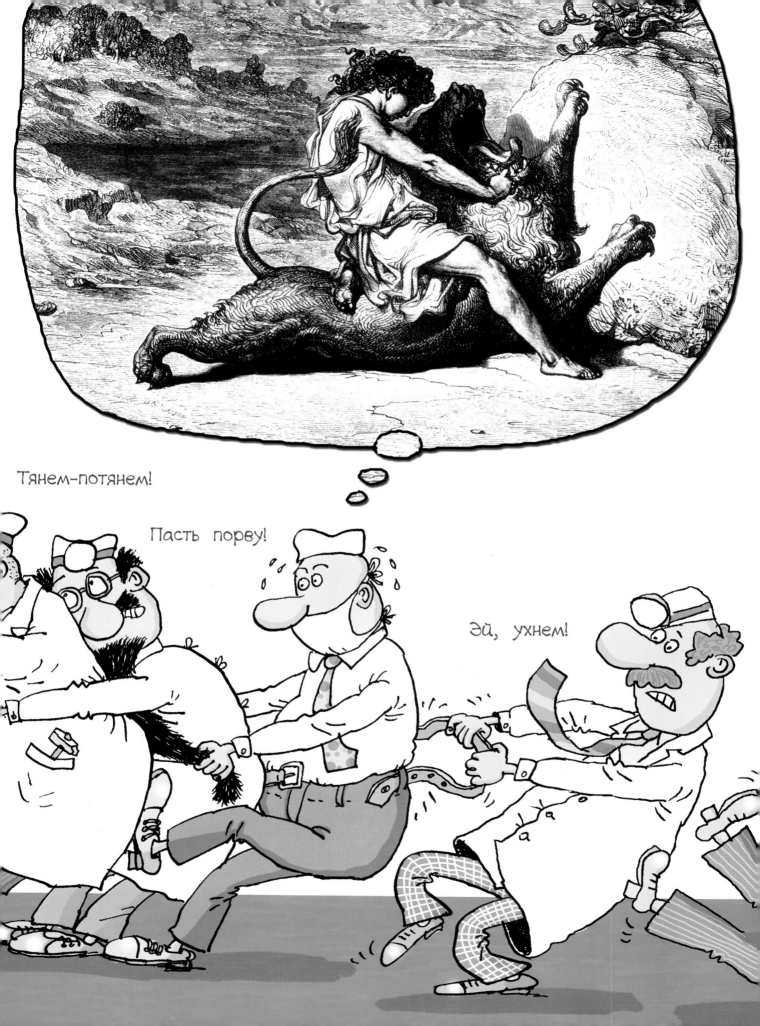

Если вы с друзьями вместе
Веселитесь во дворе,
А с утра на вас надели
Ваше новое пальто,
То не стоит ползать в лужах,
И кататься по земле,
И взбираться на заборы,
Повисая на гвоздях.
Чтоб не портить и не пачкать
Ваше новое пальто,
Нужно сделать его старым.
Это делается так:

Залезайте прямо в лужу,
Покатайтесь по земле,
И немножко на заборе
Повисите на гвоздях.
Очень скоро станет старым
Ваше новое пальто,
Вот теперь спокойно можно
Веселиться во дворе.
Можно смело ползать в лужах,
И кататься по земле,
И взбираться на заборы,
Повисая на гвоздях.

Умывальников начальник

Е сли, сына отмывая,
Обнаружит мама вдруг,
Что она не сына моет,
А чужую чью-то дочь...
Пусть не нервничает мама,
Ну не всё ли ей равно?
Никаких различий нету
Между грязными детьми.

(Эта страница ещё грязнее, чем эти дети.)

Если ты остался дома
Без родителей, один,
Предложить тебе могу я
Интересную игру
Под названьем «Смелый повар»
Или «Храбрый кулинар».
Суть игры в приготовленьи
Всевозможных вкусных блюд.
Предлагаю для начала
Вот такой простой рецепт:

Нужно в папины ботинки
Вылить мамины духи,
А потом ботинки эти
Смазать кремом для бритья,
И, полив их рыбьим жиром
С чёрной тушью пополам,
Бросить в суп, который мама
Приготовила с утра.
И варить с закрытой крышкой
Ровно семьдесят минут.
Что получится — узнаешь,
Когда взрослые придут.

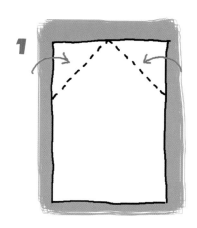 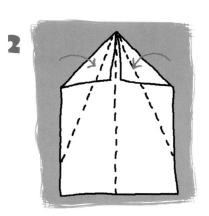 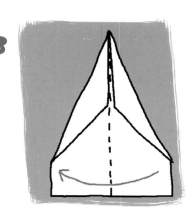

Модель реактивного самолётика для полётов на Запад.

 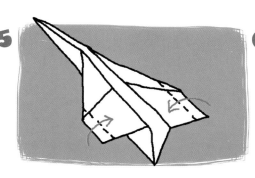 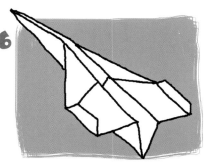

Е сли вы решили твёрдо
Самолёт угнать на Запад,
Но не можете придумать,
Чем пилотов напугать,
Почитайте им отрывки
Из сегодняшней газеты,
И они в страну любую
Вместе с вами улетят.

КУРС НА ЮГ!

Вкуснятина!
Пальчики
оближешь!

Если руки за обедом
Вы испачкали салатом
И стесняетесь о скатерть
Пальцы вытереть свои,
Опустите незаметно
Их под стол и там спокойно
Вытирайте ваши руки
Об соседские штаны.

ПЧХИ!

ТЕАТР ТЕНЕЙ

Чистыми руками можно показывать фигуры животных.

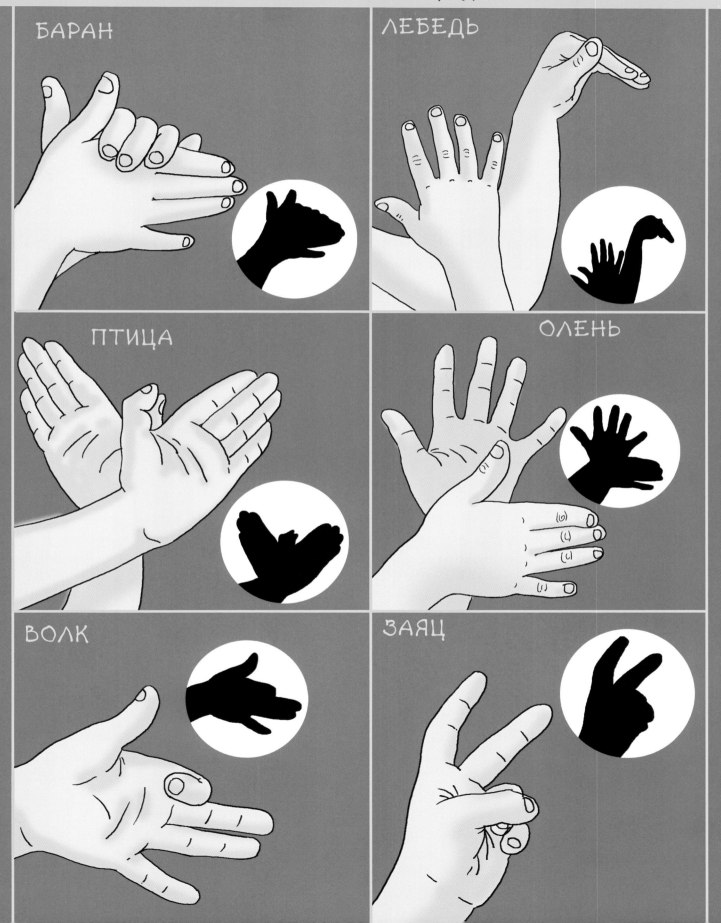

БАРАН

ЛЕБЕДЬ

ПТИЦА

ОЛЕНЬ

ВОЛК

ЗАЯЦ

Если вас зовут обедать,
Гордо прячьтесь под диван
И лежите там тихонько,
Чтоб не сразу вас нашли.
А когда из-под дивана
Будут за ноги тащить,
Вырывайтесь и кусайтесь,
Не сдавайтесь без борьбы.
Если всё-таки достанут
И за стол посадят вас,
Опрокидывайте чашку,
Выливайте на пол суп.
Зажимайте рот руками,
Падайте со стула вниз,
А котлеты вверх бросайте,
Пусть прилипнут к потолку.
Через месяц люди скажут
С уважением о вас:
«С виду он худой и дохлый,
Но зато характер твёрд».

Как

правильно держать
вилку и нож

А

Б

В

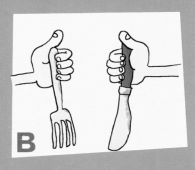

Г

Д

Если друг на день рожденья
Пригласил тебя к себе,
Ты оставь подарок дома —
Пригодится самому.
Сесть старайся рядом с тортом.
В разговоры не вступай —
Ты во время разговора
Вдвое меньше съешь конфет.
Выбирай куски помельче,
Чтоб быстрее проглотить.
Не хватай салат руками —
Ложкой больше зачерпнёшь.
Если вдруг дадут орехи,
Сыпь их бережно в карман,
Но не прячь туда варенье —
Трудно будет вынимать.

Вкуснятина!

НЯМ!
НЯМ!

Когда роняет чашку гость,
Не бейте гостя в лоб.
Другую чашку дайте, пусть
Он пьёт спокойно чай.
Когда и эту чашку гость
Уронит со стола,
В стакан налейте чай ему,
И пусть спокойно пьёт.
Когда же всю посуду гость
В квартире перебьёт,
Придётся сладкий чай налить
За шиворот ему.

Если вы собрались другу
Рассказать свою беду,
Брать за пуговицу друга
Бесполезно — убежит
И на память вам оставит
Эту пуговицу друг.
Лучше дать ему подножку,
На пол бросить, сверху сесть
И тогда уже подробно
Рассказать свою беду.

Собака — друг человека

Кто не прыгал из окошка
Вместе с маминым зонтом,
Тот лихим парашютистом
Не считается пока.
Не лететь ему, как птице,
Над взволнованной толпой,
Не лежать ему в больнице
С забинтованной ногой.

Если вы решили первым
Стать в рядах своих сограждан —
Никогда не догоняйте
Устремившихся вперёд.
Через пять минут, ругаясь,
Побегут они обратно,
И тогда, толпу возглавив,
Вы помчитесь впереди.

Посмотрите, что творится
В каждом доме по ночам.
Отвернувшись к стенке носом,
Молча взрослые лежат.
Шевелят они губами
В беспросветной темноте
И с закрытыми глазами
Пяткой дёргают во сне.

Ни за что не соглашайтесь
По ночам идти в кровать.
Никому не позволяйте
Вас укладывать в постель.
Неужели вы хотите
Годы детские свои
Провести под одеялом,
На подушке, без штанов?

Потерявшийся ребёнок
Должен помнить, что его
Отведут домой, как только
Назовёт он адрес свой.
Надо действовать умнее,
Говорите: «Я живу
Возле пальмы с обезьяной
На далёких островах».
Потерявшийся ребёнок,
Если он не дурачок,
Не упустит верный случай
В разных странах побывать.

Потерявшийся ребёнок

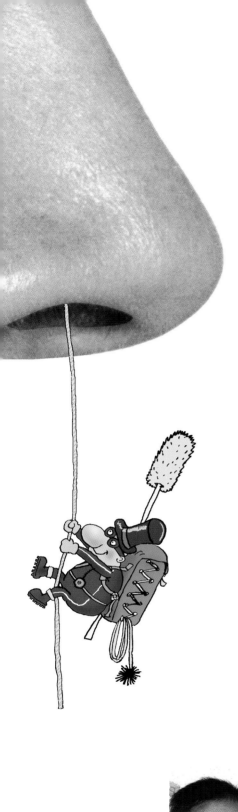

Нет приятнее занятья,
Чем в носу поковырять.
Всем ужасно интересно,
Что там спрятано внутри.
А кому смотреть противно,
Тот пускай и не глядит.
Мы же в нос к нему не лезем,
Пусть и он не пристаёт.

В XVII веке
считалось изящным
ковырять в носу
мизинцем.

«Надо с младшими делиться!».
«Надо младшим помогать!» —
Никогда не забывайте
Эти правила, друзья.
Очень тихо повторяйте
Их тому, кто старше вас,
Чтобы младшие про это
Не узнали ничего.

СТАРШИЕ и младшие. Найдите на картинках 25 отличий.

Бей друзей без передышки
Каждый день по полчаса,
И твоя мускулатура
Станет крепче кирпича.

А могучими руками,
Ты, когда придут враги,
Сможешь в трудную минуту
Защитить своих друзей.

Бейте палками лягушек.
Это очень интересно.
Отрывайте крылья мухам,
Пусть побегают пешком.
Тренируйтесь ежедневно,
И наступит день счастливый —
Вас в какое-нибудь царство
Примут главным палачом.

VIP — очень важная персона.
Король, министр, звезда шоу-бизнеса и др.

Если вы по коридору
Мчитесь на велосипеде,
А навстречу вам из ванной
Вышел папа погулять,
Не сворачивайте в кухню,
В кухне — твёрдый холодильник.
Тормозите лучше в папу.
Папа мягкий. Он простит.

КЛАССИФИКАЦИЯ ПАП

твёрдый
папа

папа
средней мягкости

мягкий
папа

84

Есть надёжный способ папу
Навсегда свести с ума:
Расскажите папе честно,
Что вы делали вчера.
Если он при этом сможет
Удержаться на ногах,
Объясните, чем заняться
Завтра думаете вы.
И когда с безумным видом
Папа песни запоёт,
Вызывайте неотложку.
Телефон её 03.

Заведи себе тетрадку
И записывай подробно,
Кто кого на переменке
Сколько раз куда послал,
С кем учитель физкультуры
Пил кефир в спортивном зале
И что папа ночью маме
Тихо на ухо шептал.

МАСКА "СЕКРЕТНЫЙ АГЕНТ"
*Вырежите дырки для глаз и носа,
наденьте и смело можете
подглядывать и подслушивать*

Рот на замке

Eсли ты пришёл к знакомым,
Не здоровайся ни с кем.
Слов: «Пожалуйста», «Спасибо»
Никому не говори.
Отвернись и на вопросы
Ни на чьи не отвечай.
И тогда никто не скажет
Про тебя, что ты болтун.

Игра в «молчанку»

враг
Здравствуйте!
Спасибо!
Пожалуйста!
Болтун-
находка
для врага!

Требуют тебя к ответу?
Что ж, умей держать ответ.
Не трясись, не хнычь, не мямли,
Никогда не прячь глаза.
Например, спросила мама:
«Кто игрушки разбросал?»
Отвечай, что это папа
Приводил своих друзей.
Ты подрался с младшим братом?
Говори, что первый он
Бил тебя ногой по шее
И ругался, как бандит.
Если спросят, кто на кухне
Все котлеты искусал,
Отвечай, что кот соседский,
А, возможно, сам сосед.
В чём бы ты ни провинился,
Научись держать ответ.
За свои поступки каждый
Должен смело отвечать.

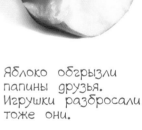

Яблоко обгрызли
папины друзья.
Игрушки разбросали
тоже они.

Кот соседский Васисуалий.
Тот ещё плутишка!

КЛЯНУСЬ!
НЕ ЕЛ Я ВАШИ
КОТЛЕТЫ!

Сосед сверху.
Ему точно верить нельзя!

Если что-нибудь случилось
И никто не виноват,
Не ходи туда, иначе
Виноватым будешь ты.
Спрячься где-нибудь в сторонке,
А потом иди домой
И про то, что видел это,
Никому не говори.

Не шали!

Если вы окно разбили,
Не спешите признаваться.
Погодите, не начнется ль
Вдруг гражданская война.
Артиллерия ударит,
Стёкла вылетят повсюду,
И никто ругать не станет
За разбитое окно.

Чтобы самовозгоранья
В доме не произошло,
Выходя из помещенья,
Уноси с собой утюг.
Пылесос, электроплитку,
Телевизор и торшер
Лучше, с лампочками вместе,
Вынести в соседний двор.
А ещё надёжней будет
Перерезать провода,
Чтоб во всём твоём районе
Сразу вырубился свет.
Тут уж можешь быть уверен
Ты почти наверняка,
Что от самовозгоранья
Дом надёжно уберёг.

НЕВОЗМОЖНО РАБОТАТЬ. Постоянно ВЫРУБАЮТ СВЕТ!

Д разниться лучше из окна,
С восьмого этажа.
Из танка тоже хорошо,
Когда крепка броня.
Но если хочешь довести
Людей до горьких слёз,
Их безопаснее всего
По радио дразнить.

Если твой сосед по парте
Стал источником заразы,
Обними его — и в школу
Две недели не придёшь.

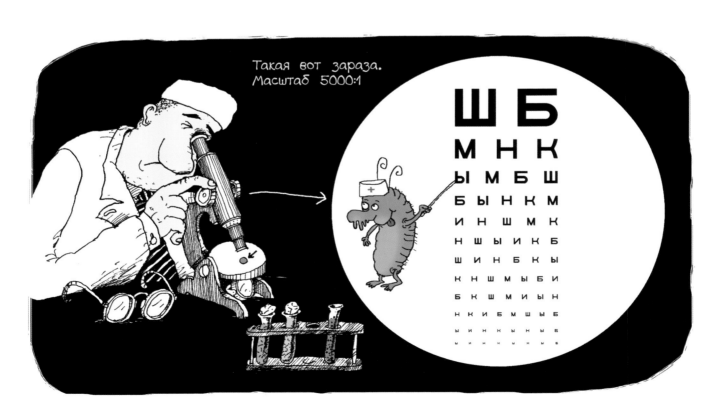

Такая вот зараза.
Масштаб 5000:1

ШБ
МНК
ЫМБШ
БЫНКМ
ИНШМК
НШЫИКБ
ШИНБКЫ
КНШМЫБИ
БКШМИЫН
НКИБМШЫБ
ЫИННЫНЫБ
ЫИНННЫНЫ

Если ты весь мир насилья
Собираешься разрушить
И при этом стать мечтаешь
Всем, не будучи ничем,
Смело двигайся за нами
По проложенной дороге,
Мы тебе дорогу эту
Можем даже уступить.

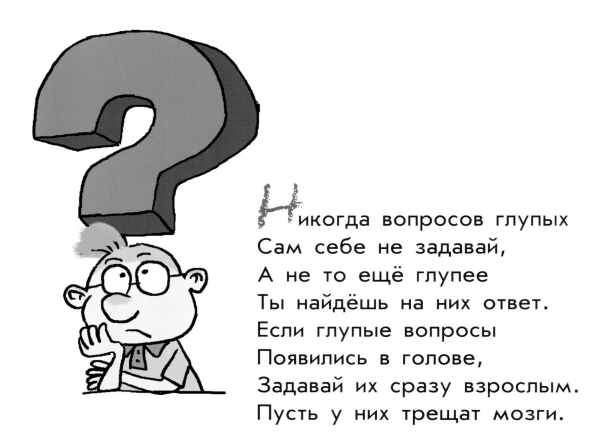

Никогда вопросов глупых
Сам себе не задавай,
А не то ещё глупее
Ты найдёшь на них ответ.
Если глупые вопросы
Появились в голове,
Задавай их сразу взрослым.
Пусть у них трещат мозги.

ГЛУПЫЕ ВОПРОСЫ
от БАЛБЕСА

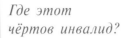

Где этот чёртов инвалид?

Вы не скажете, как пройти в библиотеку?

Вы не скажете, который час?

Вы не скажете, сколько сейчас градусов ниже нуля?

Бабуля, закурить не найдётся?

А где бабуля?

Не расстраивайтесь, если
Вызывают в школу маму
Или папу. Не стесняйтесь,
Приводите всю семью.
Пусть приходят дяди, тёти
И троюродные братья,
Если есть у вас собака,
Приводите и её.

ФРАЗЫ ИЗ ШКОЛЬНЫХ СОЧИНЕНИЙ

Во двор въехали две лошади.
Это были сыновья Тараса Бульбы.

Герасим поставил на пол блюдечко
и стал тыкать в него мордочкой.

У неё были карие глаза
с веснушками на носу.

Драпай
на предыдущую страницу!

Решил подраться — выбирай
Того, кто послабей.
А сильный может сдачи дать,
Зачем тебе она?
Чем младше тот, кого ты бьёшь,
Тем сердцу веселей
Глядеть, как плачет он, кричит
И мамочку зовёт.
Но если вдруг за малыша
Вступился кто-нибудь,
Беги, кричи, и громко плачь,
И мамочку зови.

Я БОЛЬШЕ
НЕ БУДУ!!!

МАМА!!!

УДК 821.161.1-3-053.2
ББК 84(2 Рос = Рус)6-7
О-76

Серия «Мировая классика для детей»

Литературно-художественное издание
Для младшего школьного возраста

Григорий Бенционович Остер

ВРЕДНЫЕ СОВЕТЫ

Художник Н. Воронцов

Дизайн обложки *Н. Сушковой*
Редактор *С. Младова*
Художественный редактор *О. Ведерников*
Технический редактор *Е. Кудиярова*
Корректор *И. Мокина*
Компьютерная вёрстка *Н. Воронцов*

Подписано в печать 28.07.2017
Формат 60×84 / 8. Печать офсетная. Усл. печ. л. 14,0.
Доп. тираж 2 000 экз. Заказ № 4101

ООО «Издательство АСТ»
129085, РФ, г. Москва, Звёздный бульвар,
дом 21, стр. 1, ком. 39
Наш электронный адрес: www.ast.ru

«Баспа Аста» деген ООО.
129085 г. Мәскеу, жұлдызды гүлзар, д. 21, 1 құрылым, 39 бөлме
Біздің электрондық мекенжайымыз: www.ast.ru. E-mail: malysh@ast.ru
Қазақстан Республикасында дистрибьютор және өнім бойынша
арыз-талаптарды қабылдаушының өкілі
«РДЦ-Алматы» ЖШС, Алматы қ., Домбровский көш., 3«а», литер Б, офис 1.
Тел.: 8(727) 251 59 89,90,91,92, факс: 8 (727) 251 58 12 вн. 107;
E-mail: RDC-Almaty@eksmo.kz
Өнімнің жарамдылық мерзімі шектелмеген.
Өндірген мемлекет: Ресей. Сертификация қарастырылған

Общероссийский классификатор продукции ОК-005-93, том 2;
953000—книги, брошюры
Отпечатано с электронных носителей издательства.
ОАО "Тверской полиграфический комбинат". 170024, г. Тверь, пр-т Ленина, 5.

Остер, Григорий Бенционович.

О-76   Вредные советы : [стихи] / Г. Остер; ил. Н. Воронцов. — Москва : Издательство АСТ, 2017. — 110, [2] с.: ил. — (Мировая классика для детей).

ISBN 978-5-17-087434-7.

«Вредные советы» для детсадовцев и младших школьников. Для тех, кто рисует на обоях, купается в лужах и вообще отличается в быту необузданным поведением.
Автор в представлении не нуждается.
Для младшего школьного возраста.

УДК 821.161.1-3-053.2
ББК 84(2 Рос = Рус)6-7

6+

ЕАС

ТОВАРИЩИ РОДИТЕЛИ!

Штраф за безобразное поведение вашего ребёнка Вы можете оплатить в любой сберкассе города.

Homecoming Quilts

Celebrating Scotland's Textiles, Quilts and Quiltmakers

Loch Maree by Effie Galletly

by Ruth Higham, Patricia Macindoe and Isabel Paterson

Published by Loch Lomond Quilt Show Ltd

www.lochlomondquiltshow.com

Scotland's year of Homecoming celebrates many of Scotland's great contributions to the world, and offers an invitation to the millions of people around the globe who have an ancestral link or a love for the country to come back and visit Scotland in 2009.

The Loch Lomond Quilt Show is Scotland's annual international celebration of patchwork and quilting.

In the pages of this book we've brought the two things together in a celebration of the textiles of Scotland seen through its quilts and quiltmakers.

Homecoming Quilts has been made possible through funding from Homecoming Scotland.

2009

This book is dedicated to:

Alistair, Chris and Richard
Makepeace Quilters
The Quilters of Scotland

This book is published by the Loch Lomond Quilt Show Ltd

The Studio, Unit 14, Griffon Centre, Vale of Leven Industrial Estate, Dumbarton, G82 3PD

The right of Ruth Higham, Patricia Macindoe and Isabel Paterson to be identified as the Authors of this Work has been asserted by them in accordance with the Copyright, Designs and Patents Act 1988.

ISBN 978-0-9562324-0-3
British Library Cataloguing in Publication Data
A catalogue record for this book is available from the British Library

Designed and edited by Teamwork, Christopher & Gail Lawther, 100 Wiston Avenue, Worthing, West Sussex, England BN14 7PS thelawthers@ntlworld.com

Printed by Paterson Printing Ltd, Tunbridge Wells, Kent (www.patersons.com)

Contents

Introduction by Janet Rae

QUILTMAKERS in Scotland benefit from a wide range of influences and a unique textile heritage.

First of all, and to start with colour as many textile artists do, they have the varied palette of the natural environment as inspiration. Take the lush green of Galloway and mix with the purple, yellow, brown and grey of the Highlands. Add in the differing hues of the surrounding sea and you have a starting point. The built environment adds its own bit of emphasis: grey granite and slates, red sandstone tenements and pantile roofs, white and pastel-coloured cottages along a seafront – the colour is there in abundance.

Design is the next important ingredient, and it is preceded by 'know-how.' Although the quilt revival of the 1960s and 1970s brought an influx of quilt patterns and techniques from the United States, historical research has proven that many of these traditions started on this side of the Atlantic and migrated with the settlers. Quilts have been made in Scotland for several hundred years, but often within the context of other disciplines: a utilitarian bedcover in a Highland croft made of offcuts from the loom owed more to the weaver than the quilter per se, while exquisite silk or crewel flowers on a quilted ground would probably have been the work of a dedicated embroiderer. Both are deemed to be 'quilts.'

Competency with the needle(s) is a Scottish legacy that embraces more than patchwork. It encompasses a range of utilitarian and decorative textile pursuits that include knitting, weaving, tapestry and embroidery. The embroidery tradition itself goes back in time to the 16th century and Mary Queen of Scots. Mary was, however, taught her skills at the French Court and throughout her long periods of imprisonment had a French 'imbroiderer' to draw her designs. Over succeeding centuries other men and women of a lesser social standing were driven to produce textiles more by necessity than art; some of their distinctive garments continue to this day. In terms of native Scottish patterns, mention 'Shetland,' 'Fair Isle,' 'Eriskay' and 'Sanquhar,' and you immediately conjure up indigenous design.

Education made its own contribution to Scotland's textile development and design. Early schools inevitably included provision to teach girls the basics: how to knit and turn a collar. In the 18th and 19th centuries, the pupils at Edinburgh schools for daughters of the gentry learned fancy needlework and other things which might qualify them to become good housekeepers. The later colleges of domestic science would also have taught some basic stitching skills, and then there were the art schools – particularly in Glasgow and Dundee.

Weaving and embroidery perpetuated traditional hand skills, but the addition of design moved textiles forward and into art. Gifted teachers made their mark on future generations – people such as Ann Macbeth who, with Margaret Swanson (both instructors at Glasgow School of Art) co-authored *Educational Needlecraft* in 1911. This textbook had profound influence in Scotland and abroad, especially in Canada and Japan. Along with the practical instructions about patching, tucking, French seams and even making knickers, there was guidance on pattern and design – on working with straight lines and circles, the use of the leaf form and decorative appliqué for ages 14 to 24! Above all else was the message that students must create their own designs. The ethos of Jessie Newbery, who had started 'Art Needlework' and GSA's first Embroidery Class in 1894, was spread far and wide.

The art colleges today still lead with innovation in textile design and up-to-date technology, in Glasgow, Dundee and Galashiels. Computers with graphic design, illustration and Photoshop capabilities, as well as the advent of digital textile printing, have changed the way individual artists work, and also mass production techniques.

Scottish quilters are also fortunate to have a legacy linked to the manufacture of many different kinds of cloth, though sadly not much of this manufacturing is done today. The former production of linen and blankets, woollen serge and twill, and the bright Turkey Red cottons, which occupied so many looms in the West of Scotland in the late 18th century to the beginning of the 20th, are all part of this textile mix, as are Paisley shawls. Add to this tweed (which became mechanised in the Scottish Borders in 1820), and Harris Tweed, which was introduced in the Western Hebrides

about 1850, and is still made by self-employed weavers. The ubiquitous tartan itself will most certainly continue as long as there are tourists and Burns' suppers – who can best a handmade kilt, or a fine cashmere or lambswool sweater from a Borders mill?

Homecoming evokes many thoughts and memories – especially for those Scots who will return to their country in 2009. For Scottish quiltmakers who have come of age in the last 30 years, and stayed 'at home,' there is a different type of appreciation. I like to think that each of today's Scottish quiltmakers stands at the front of a very long queue that stretches back through generations of gifted textile experts, artists and manufacturers, each of whom has made his or her own particular contribution to textile heritage. They have provided the initiative and the inspiration – it is up to the present textile enthusiasts to carry it forward.
© Janet Rae

A Rich Heritage

SCOTLAND is a country rich in beauty, natural resources and its people; the people of Scotland are rich in ideas, inventiveness and talent. Over the centuries many of those ideas have made Scotland a centre of innovation in industry, thought and literature. One of the industries for which Scotland became famous was textile production: tartans, Harris Tweed, Turkey Red dyed fabrics, Paisley shawls, Coats cotton thread and Ayrshire Whitework form just some of Scotland's textile heritage.

By the 12th century wool was already an important economic factor in Scotland. Wool finished in Scotland was coloured using local natural dyes; it was these variations of colour in the simple warp and weft woven cloth that would develop into tartan. The colours once dyed began to take on recognisable differences, and so became associated with various clans and areas. The wearing of tartans was banned during the Jacobite revolution, but become popular again during Victorian times. The Highland Clearances of the 19th century were partly so that more sheep, and therefore more wool, could be produced. A huge Scottish diaspora resulted, with many Scots leaving for North America.

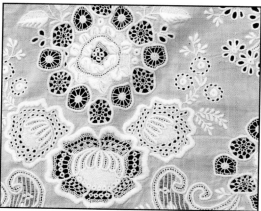

Top: *Patricia took this photograph at a sale at The Tweed Mill, P&J Haggarty Ltd, Aberfeldy, Perthshire*
Above: *Ayrshire Whitework, courtesy of writer and collector Catherine Czerkawska. A gown probably made in Maybole, Ayrshire. It belonged to a Peggy McGawn and was known as the 'McGregor family gown'. http://www.wordarts.blogspot.com/*

ABOVE: *Tartans ancient and modern*

BELOW: *An old Harris Tweed jacket*

Harris Tweed was made on the islands of Harris, Lewis, Barra and Uist. Although it was originally made to be worn by locals, a market for the hard-wearing cloth outside the islands developed in the mid 19th century. The making of Harris Tweed survives today.

Two of Scotland's most famous sons had connections to the textile trade in Scotland. Andrew Carnegie, industrialist and philanthropist, was born into a weaving family in Dunfermline in 1835; his first job was as a bobbin boy, changing spools of thread at a cotton mill. David Livingstone, explorer, worked in the Montieth, Bogle & Co Mill in Blantyre. This factory used the Turkey Red process of dyeing fabrics, producing the Montieth handkerchief – exported all around the world – eventually becoming known as the bandanna. Turkey Red is important as the first really colour-fast red dye. During the 19th century the industrialisation of

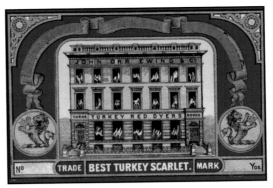

LEFT: *Turkey Red samples and trade labels from the Collection of West Dunbartonshire Council. The top right sample shows the trademark of John Orr Ewing & Co.*

cotton spinning, weaving and dyeing brought a huge increase in the numbers of factories and mills.

The Turkey Red industry soon moved many of its factories and dye works to the Vale of Leven, a beautiful valley between the river Clyde and the foot of Loch Lomond. The locals became known as 'jellie eaters' as their hands became stained red with the dyes as though they had been making or eating jam. Turkey Red cotton was exported all over the world, and very quickly became popular with quiltmakers because of its colour-fast qualities.

Paisley shawls were named after the industrial town south of the Clyde where they were produced, although Paisley was neither the originator of the idea nor the only place that the shawls were made. By the latter part of the 19th century, though, so many shawls were produced there that most people referred to them as Paisley shawls. In Jen Jones' collection of Welsh quilts there are a number that have used old Paisley shawls as a backing or as part of the design – and of course the Paisley pattern remains a perennial favourite motif in printed fabrics.

Along with the industrial side of textile production, Scotland has a history of making fine hand textiles. Ayrshire Whitework is a drawn-thread technique using white thread on a white muslin base. Fine muslin was produced in Ayrshire from the 18th century onwards; the embroidery on the muslin produced work with a lace-like quality, making it especially popular for christening dresses.

A Love of Design

RIGHT: *Paisley Shawl Design DCC39 from The Glasgow School of Art Archives and Collections. The blank area on the right shows where the next repeat of the design tucks into the first motif.*

THE making of clothing, household linens and decorative needlework are universal skills. Once the basic requirements of clothing (warmth and protection) have been taken care of, and household textiles have been produced for utility and privacy, it seems to be part of human nature to add decoration and individuality.

Most of Scotland's early textile history will have been based around hearth and home, with young girls learning how to make clothing and household linens. There will always have been professional tailors, seamstresses, embroiderers, knitters and lace makers, but most of the work would have been done by those who needed it. With needlework, as with many domestic crafts, very little is recorded of who made what: only wealthy families, who are survived by wills and domestic inventories, left any indications of what skills were used around the home. Textiles rot and wear with use, so many ordinary things are simply worn away: only the exceptional and precious survive, and not many of them.

It was with the rise of the industrial and the commercial worlds that textile education became formalised. Scotland has added much to the industrial processes needed to make cloth, but we must not forget at the same time how much Scotland added to the design, colour and style of what it produced. Tartans have as much colour and variation as the clans they represent. Harris Tweeds come in an extraordinary range of colours. The Turkey Red pattern books in the collection of West Dunbartonshire Council have to be seen to be believed: endless variations in stunning colours.

In the same way that technology has always informed design, the desire to

produce certain designs has inspired technology. What is possible in thread and fabric production has also inspired the craft and art makers of the textile world in turn. From its very inception (in 1845), Glasgow School of Art (GSA) has been linked with excellence in textile design; indeed its first board of directors deliberately included representatives of textile manufacturers from Paisley, Turkey Red, calico printing etc to provide the link between technology and the need for well-designed products.

The Embroidery and Needlework Department at GSA started in 1894 with Jessie Newbery at its head. It studied the techniques and styles of the past, and of other cultures, but always with an eye (and hand) on developing the style, not imitating it.

'I believe in education consisting of seeing the best that has been done. Then having this high standard before us, in doing

Inspirational cover from Needlework Development Scheme pamphlet

what we like to do: that for our fathers, this for us.' Jessie Newbery in 1898. (quoted from p5, *Textile Treasures at the Glasgow School of Art* by Liz Arthur, Glasgow School of Art Press, 2005).

The School of Textile Design at Galashiels (part of Heriot-Watt University), Duncan of Jordanstone at Dundee University, Gray's School of Art in Aberdeen, GSA, and Edinburgh College of Art, all have fine reputations in textiles studies (both for industrial and fine art practitioners) that have carried on into the 21st century. Frances Stevenson MA, Programmes Director for Textiles at Dundee, says 'Students are currently working on quilt ideas for a competition run by the V&A; the winner will have their work hung as part of a major quilt exhibition in 2010.'

It was one of Scotland's great industrial companies that provided craft and art textile education in the 20th century. J&P Coats Ltd of Paisley was formed in 1830 to produce thread for home and industrial uses. By the early part of the 20th century, Coats realised that the home sewing market was slowly decreasing, because of the availability of ready-to-wear clothes and ready-made household linens, so they anonymously founded the Needlework Development Scheme. This trained and funded teachers of craft needlework, funded pamphlets and the *Needlewoman* magazine, and sponsored the collection

Deconstructed Streak O' Lightning

Patricia (centre in the photograph below right) has great fun working on a quilt project with 'conceptual artists in the making,' a group of Sculpture & Environmental Art students at Glasgow School of Art. The result is a configuration of red and white blocks that have been negotiated into a contemporary interpretation of a Streak O' Lightning quilt top – which will undoubtably be quilted in an equally unorthodox way.

of wonderful examples of needlework from around the world along with contemporary Scottish work. The scheme ran from 1934–1962. This subtle but effective marketing tool maintained their market in embroidery and sewing threads by encouraging the home users and professionals alike.

Textiles in the 21st century have memory, can cool or heat their environment, light up, reflect light and project images. They can be made in the most traditional of ways or with no human involvement, and can be cut by hand or by laser; they can be stitched by hand or machine, or have no stitching at all. High tech or low tech – which will have the greater influence over our quiltmaking in the next few decades?

Scottish Quiltmaking

QUILTMAKING in Scotland was probably born out of the same necessities as elsewhere. The needs to keep warm in a cold climate, to join and layer textiles to increase their thermal properties, and to use and reuse precious resources will all have contributed to the birthing process.

'We made haaps ti make use o' the worn blaankets – ye coundna' throw them oot.' Daisy Atchison, former herring girl from Eyemouth 1985, quoted from a personal conversation with Dorothy Osler in Dorothy's book *Traditional British Quilts* (Batsford, 1987). In this wonderful book, the chapter on Scottish Quilts is very short, just five pages – was this a sign that not many quilts were made north of the border, or that the research had yet to be done? Thankfully the latter seems to be true; other writers such as Janet Rae, in more recently-published books, seem to be able to provide more evidence.

One of the perennial problems is that quilts are not seen either as art or as important domestic items. Textiles cannot be left on permanent display in museum collections because they are damaged by light, dust and handling, so often they are consigned to storage areas where they lay semi-forgotten. Just as often when they are handed in to museums they come with almost no provenance, and no-one makes much of an effort to discover and record the little information that may be available. No-one seems to know the whole story: which Scottish museums have quilts, and what quilts do they have? There's a lot of work still to do.

Ruth Higham and Patricia Macindoe held a series of discovery days in West Dunbartonshire libraries before the first Loch Lomond Quilt Show, looking for quilts made by local people and hoping that, just maybe, they would find quilts with Turkey Red fabrics in them. It was in

BELOW: *Log Cabin quilt with Turkey Red fabrics. Made in the early 20th century from locally-dyed fabrics, this quilt is still owned by the family that made it.*

RIGHT: *Turkey Red and white Log Cabin quilt owned by Liz Stewart*

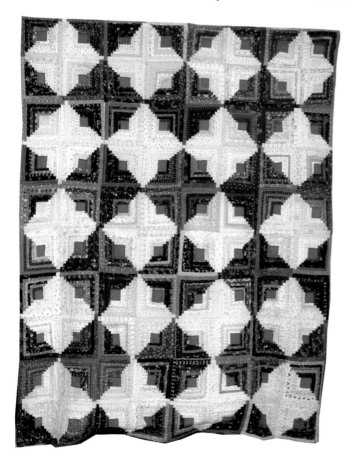

TOP RIGHT: Detail of a quilt from Hawick in the collection of Gillian Rose; the distinctive heart motifs can be seen in the border design.

BELOW RIGHT: Freddie's Trousers: made in 2005 by Ruth Higham for her husband, Richard, from his late father's suit trousers. Inspired by wool quilts seen in the Burrell.

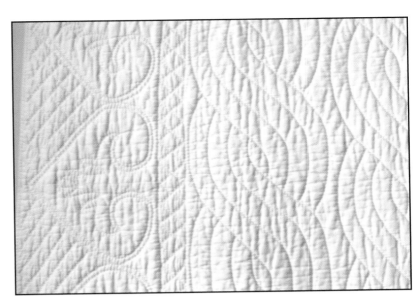

some ways a soul-destroying experience: 'We use granny's quilts for the dog;' 'When my mother died we threw them out,' and 'They were very old-fashioned so we didn't think anyone would be interested' were among the comments. No value had been placed on the quilts, so no-one thought they were important. There is a happy ending to this story, though, as several quilts were found and recorded: two are featured on the opposite page.

The Log Cabin pattern is seen in both of these quilts – perhaps not such a surprise after reading Janet Rae and Dinah Travis' book *Making Connections – Around the World with Log Cabin*. In the book they trace the history of this pattern around the world and show evidence that Northern Europe – especially Scotland, Northern Ireland and the Isle of Man – may be able to call this pattern their own.

Scotland does have some distinctive quilts. Wholecloth quilts found in and around the border town of Hawick feature distinctive quilting patterns of hearts and fleurs-de-lys. In 2008 the Quilters' Guild showed a small collection of Hawick quilts at the Festival of Quilts.

There are also some wonderful quilts in the Burrell collection: one shows the work of Colour Sergeant R Cumming. His multi-coloured patchwork made up of 1in squares of uniform fabric was made in the 1880s, and was first exhibited in 1890. Also in Glasgow Museums and Art Galleries' collection is an inlay patchwork quilt made over 18 years by John Monro of Paisley.

These and many other quilts demonstrate that quilting in many forms has been part of life in Scotland over the centuries.

A Quilting Revival

RIGHT FROM TOP:
Uplifted by Sheena Norquay; Effie Galletly's Abandoned House; A quilt by Frieda Oxenham, which was displayed in the West Kirk, LLQS 2007

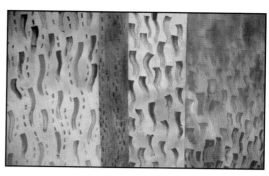

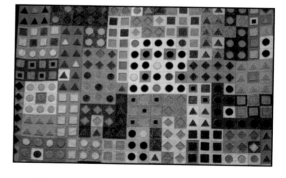

SCOTTISH quilters occasionally feel as though they are part of a secret, underground movement. 'I'm sorry; did you say you make kilts?' has been heard on more than one occasion. Happily, nothing could be further from the truth: there are many quilters is Scotland. The Guild has over 700 Scottish members, which indicates (on the iceberg principle) that there may be 7,000 ++ quilters in the country.

Scottish quilters are a tenacious, tough and well-travelled group. For Guild Regional Days, and for classes at the Studio, Dumbarton, there are women who regularly travel over 70 miles to attend. Wherever there are quilters gathering in the UK, the number of Scottish quilters is always proportionally higher than those from other areas.

The revival in quiltmaking in Scotland echoes the worldwide revival in quiltmaking that started slowly in the 1950/60s and really took off in the 1970s. What had been seen as a dying craft rose from the ashes with new tools (rotary cutters etc), new techniques (fast cutting and piecing ideas), new fabrics (specially-designed quilting fabrics and waddings), plus new ideas and new quiltmakers.

The first Scottish Guild meeting took place in Edinburgh at the Balmoral Hotel with a few dedicated enthusiasts. Jacqueline Atkinson (Glasgow) remembers: 'Those early Guild meetings were exciting for bringing people together – in particular for realising just how many people shared your enthusiasm; for those of us who had been patchworking for a long time in isolation it was a revelation.' It was the same for other members such as Sheena Norquay and Sally Watson.

For many quilters the joy and enthusiasm for the craft of making traditional quilts has stayed with them for the last 30–40 years. For others that craft has developed into an art form expressed through the

medium of textiles. The rich variety of techniques, styles and personal expression is what has kept quiltmaking interesting and alive.

Scotland has produced some renowned quilters, who have exhibited around the world and spread their knowledge and skills by teaching.

One well-known Scottish quilter, Patricia Archibald, started quilting at the age of 11, then as a young newlywed she made small quilts to sell. She later opened Purely Patchwork in Linlithgow, and after winning a business scholarship was able to travel to Houston to what was at that time the world's largest quilt show and

BELOW: *Piece of 1970s hexagon patchwork, made from furnishing fabrics – recognisable as the starting point for many quilters in the 1970s*

trade event. 'I was astounded at what could be done with fabric in an artistic, abstract and representational way.'

Many have combined working full time with making, teaching, exhibiting and talking about their work. Sheena Norquay was until recently a teacher as well as a professional quilter, producing wonderful work with a uniquely Scottish flavour. Pauline Burbidge has produced an amazing body of work, but has had to work almost as hard at securing exhibitions, funding and the business side of being a professional practitioner.

Exhibiting groups often give both peer support and encouragement to their members. Over the last few years Scotland has seen groups such as Turning Point, Free Wheeling and the Filanderers add their own perspectives to what quilting is in the 21st Century.

Quilting shops have increased in number, supporting the quilters both with fabrics and equipment, and often with a good range of classes. Local groups such as Paisley Patchers, and Helensburgh & District Quilters, have celebrated more than 20 years of successful existence. Sadly, formal courses such as City & Guilds seem almost to have died a death in colleges, but other centres such as the Studio, Dumbarton, hope to take up that mantle.

The word ordinary is invidious, but so many quilters in Scotland regard themselves as 'just an ordinary quilter.' Many, many wonderful quilts are made by the 'ordinary quilters;' women and men who don't always have much time to give to

ABOVE: Alexandria Parish Church, Balloch, LLQS 2008, showing the work of Pat Archibald

LEFT: Turning Point exhibiting at the 2008 Festival of Quilts, NEC, Birmingham

BACK ROW: Margaret O'Gorman, Liz Ferguson, Morven Roche, Joyce Watson
FRONT ROW: Jan Watson, Mary Ennis, Margaret Morrow, Pat Archibald, Jess Morrison

their passion for textiles, but who carefully make outstanding pieces of work. Many 'ordinary quilters' turn out to be talented teachers, who influence the next generation of quiltmakers by passing on their considerable skills and know-how. Many 'ordinary quilters' make an extraordinary number of quilts for voluntary organisations such as Comfort Quilts Scotland, Project Linus UK, and local groups who give to local charities.

Let's not talk about the ordinary quilters, but the *extraordinary* quilters of Scotland.

LEFT: Freya Upton entered her first competition in 2007, aged 9. In 2008 she won first prize in the 9-11 year olds category at the Festival of Quilts show. Her future plans include quilting, living the 'River Cottage' life, and driving a VW camper van.

A Quilt Show is Born

ABOVE: *Patricia, Isabel and Ruth working hard to promote the Show before it started in 2005*

RIGHT: *Janice Gunner made this piece to hang in her exhibition at the West Kirk at LLQS 2008. It was inspired by a visit there in 2007*

BELOW: *Welsh quilts from Jen Jones' collection, hanging in St Augustine's Church, LLQS 2008*

BELOW RIGHT: *A quilt from the LLQS 30 of the Best exhibition in Jamestown Parish Church, 2006*

THE LOCH LOMOND QUILT SHOW was born out of the dream of three quilters: Patricia Macindoe, Isabel Paterson and Ruth Higham.

Patricia, Isabel and Ruth began quilting together in 1997; it started almost by accident. Ruth had just started her City & Guilds in Patchwork and Quilting at Cardonald Collage in Glasgow. Patricia, already an accomplished needlewoman, had helped Ruth find the course at Cardonald, and was always very interested to see what Ruth was stitching. As Ruth stitched away during the sermons in church, Isabel also became interested in the odd things she seemed to be making. So the three of them started to meet at Ruth's house on a Wednesday evening to sew, to drink wine and to talk! Makepeace Quilters was born, and still meets every Wednesday night at the Studio in Dumbarton.

Makepeace Quilters grew as Patricia, Isabel and Ruth became more and more fascinated by all things to do with patchwork and quilting. The three of them often talked of wanting to use their love of quilting to put something back into the community in which they lived – but how?

A trip to visit old friends in Alsace, France, coincided with a visit to the Carrefour du Patchwork in St Marie Aux Mines in September 2002. The multi-sited show

started ideas rolling. Why couldn't the same style of show, using many venues and in several places, work in the Dumbarton area? Somehow the Dumbarton Quilt Show didn't quite work as a name – but the Loch Lomond Quilt Show sounded great!

Two years of hard work followed. Patricia worked very hard to persuade local churches that they could be used as exhibition spaces, Isabel used her organisational skills to hold all the details together, and Ruth talked to everyone and anyone who would listen. Families and friends were encouraging, but it wasn't until Marie Louise Mundie, a quilting friend from Helensburgh, offered some financial support that the show was finally off the ground.

There were three simple objectives for the show:

- to highlight the wonderful work of the quilters of Scotland
- to bring exciting exhibitions to Scotland
- and to celebrate Scottish textile heritage.

In 2005 the first show took place. The '30 of the Best' Exhibition was conceived to show the work of local quilters, from Helensburgh & District Quilters, Paisley Patchers and the newly-formed Glasgow Gathering of Quilters. This exhibition continues each year to highlight the work of Scottish Quilters from different areas around Scotland.

Individual Scottish quilters such as Sheena Norquay, Patricia Archibald, Georgina Chapman, Frieda Oxenham, Evelyn Ramsey and Maureen Arnott have shown their work over the years. The Quilters' Guild Region 16 (Scotland) have always been offered free space at the show in support of their work. Each three years a charitable quilting organization has been selected and supported with a free area at the show; so far Project Linus UK and Comfort Quilts Scotland have benefited.

Exhibitions from the rest of the UK and Europe have included Asa Wettre's 'Old Swedish Quilts,' Hungarian Blue and White Quilts, By Design, Colour FX, Janice Gunner, Nikki Tinkler, Lilian Hedley, Effie Galletly, Clyde Olliver and the European Art Quilts – the list goes on.

Scottish textile history has been celebrated with Turkey Red quilts, early machine-made quilts, Welsh Quilts featuring Paisley Shawls from Jen Jones' collection, Log Cabin quilts and more.

The show is much more than just its exhibits. The volunteers are considered to be among the most helpful, knowledgeable and friendly anywhere in the known quilting world. Visitors have been invited to local quilters' houses, given lifts to out-of-the-way places, comforted when distressed, and even prayed with when requested in one of the churches. Local churches provide teas, coffees and wonderful home baking,

Above: *Busy Baltimore students at the Studio*

Left: *The Studio itself*

soups and sandwiches. The social events are relaxed and fun, with Isabel and her husband Chris entertaining visitors with traditional songs on the cruise around Loch Lomond, and men in kilts supplied free at the Friday night Ceilidh.

With Loch Lomond as its gorgeous backdrop, interesting church buildings as its exhibition areas, loyal traders and devoted visitors, the Show has become one of the focal points of the quilting year in Scotland, attracting visitors and competition entries from around the world.

The Show now has an office, storage and – significantly – a workshop to hold year-round classes in: the Studio, just off the A82, near Dumbarton. Ruth, Patricia and Isabel hope that the Studio and the Show are centres for excellence in Scottish patchwork and quilting, constantly innovating, energizing and promoting all that is best in the quilting scene.

Homecoming Quilts

INSPIRED BY SCOTLAND'S YEAR OF HOMECOMING in 2009, the Loch Lomond Quilt Show designed an exhibition and a book called *Homecoming Quilts*. At the same time the Quilters' Guild of the British Isles, Region 16, which represents the Scottish members of the Guild, was also inspired by the Homecoming theme to produce a Tartan Holdall Collection. These two projects came together to become one of the 2009 exhibitions at the Loch Lomond Quilt Show.

Scotland called out to the blood and heart Scots around the world to come home and celebrate the unique spirit of Scotland in 2009. Many men and women around the world claim a direct bloodline back to the highlands and lowlands of Scotland. It is also wonderful to know how many people also feel their heart strings pulled by the lure of a country to which they have no direct link.

This idea of Homecoming sowed the seeds of a special focus for the 2009 LLQS. Quiltmakers from outside Scotland were invited to make and send quilts, and give an insight into what Scotland means to them. Selected quilts would 'come home' to Scotland to be part of the exhibition. Alongside the Homecoming Quilts, people would be able to see glimpses of Scotland's historic quilts. The organisers would also appeal to anyone with an old quilt tucked away to have it recorded and photographed so

that a more complete picture can be formed about historic quilts made in Scotland.

The exhibition would also include the new Tartan Holdall Collection from Region 16 of the Quilters' Guild of the British Isles, and some of the Inspired by Scotland quilts seen in this book.

The 'insider' and 'outsider' views of Scotland recorded in quilts combine to give a wonderful insight into the history, heritage, myths, legends, flora, fauna and textiles – as well as the character – of the people of Scotland. The Year of Homecoming has been celebrated in so many ways: through dance and song, through theatre and concerts, through sport and outdoor pastimes, and now through quilts.

The Homecoming Quilts exhibition and book have been funded through Homecoming Scotland. The Loch Lomond Quilt Show directors, Scottish quilters and visiting quiltmakers are grateful for a chance to celebrate Scotland in this unique way.

Massachussets, USA # Fiona Wysocki

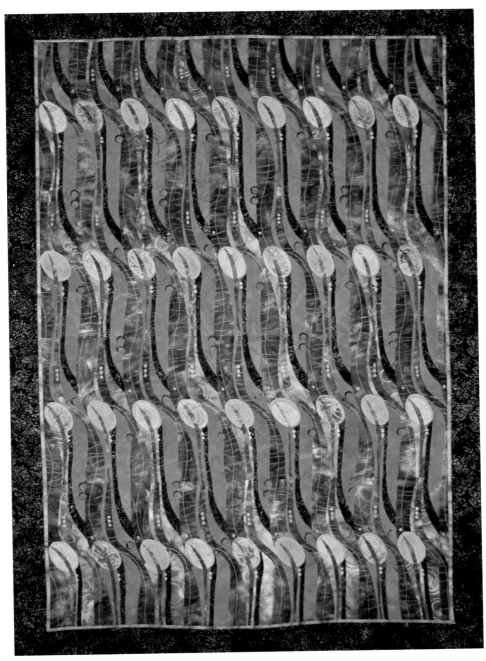

Tiptoe Through the Tulips

56in (142cm) high, 43in (109cm) wide

Inspired by Charles Rennie Mackintosh's *Stylized Tulips Sketch*, in the collection of the Hunterian Museum and Art Gallery, University of Glasgow

Techniques

Machine piecing, raw-edge appliqué, machine embroidery and machine quilting.

INSPIRATION

I live overseas but am lucky enough to return to Scotland often each year to visit family. I wanted to make a quilt that represented the beauty I see when I go home: the fields of yellow rapeseed, the gray waters of our burns, the hills and trees.

I studied at Dundee Art School, and as a child went to Saturday drawing classes at the Glasgow School of Art. From these surroundings I discovered the works of Charles Rennie Mackintosh. I wanted to create a quilt to blend the colors that remind me of Scotland in an *homage* to Mackintosh. For me, it's a natural landscape of the colors of heather, rapeseed, rhododendrons and rivers. Though tulips aren't necessarily Scottish I think Mackintosh would have liked their visual appeal in this quilt.

Monique Martin Goult, France

**Ciselures
('Chiselling')**

*44in (112cm) high,
41in (104cm) wide*

Techniques

I think I invented this method, using as the basis Richelieu embroidery and Matisse-style leaves on an appliqué quilt.

INSPIRATION

I study 'transparency' in quilts; this one is the first I've actually made. As I created the cutwork I thought I could use an adaptation of the method, incorporating veil or sheer fabric between the sandwiched layers. After I'd cut away all the layers except the sheer fabric, I assembled the quilt with satin stitch. When photographed against the light, the solid fabrics create a darker frame around the translucent sheer shapes. These organic forms are reminiscent of the ferns and mosses in Scottish glens.

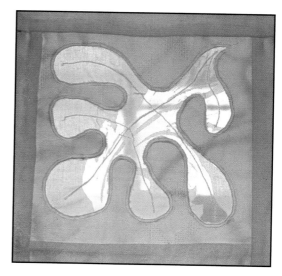

Virginia, USA Marjo Mullins

**Mull of Kintyre
Calling to Me**

*46in (117.5cm) high,
31in (80cm) wide*

Techniques

Machine piecing,
hand quilting with
light embellishment
and embroidery.
Cotton and cotton-
blend fabrics.

INSPIRATION

After longing to see Scotland since I was a child, my dream came true in 2008 when I got to visit for two weeks. Everywhere we went my senses absorbed the beauty of the country and the warmth of the people. On a clear Sunday morning I stood on the rough hillside above the Mull of Kintyre lighthouse, looking across the ocean to Ireland's Rathlin Island lighthouse. I felt my whole life had been directed to that place and I had come home, as I could hear *Mull of Kintyre* singing in my mind.

Lauren Garwood Norfolk, England

Rest in Peace

76in (193cm) high,
53in (135cm) wide

Techniques

All-white machine quilted bedspread with floral appliqué, beading detail and scent pockets. Following a theme of integrated pattern and texture, using my own screen-printed fabrics. The two details of the quilt (right, and below right) show different techniques I've used, and the third photograph shows a stitched sample taken from my sketchbook.

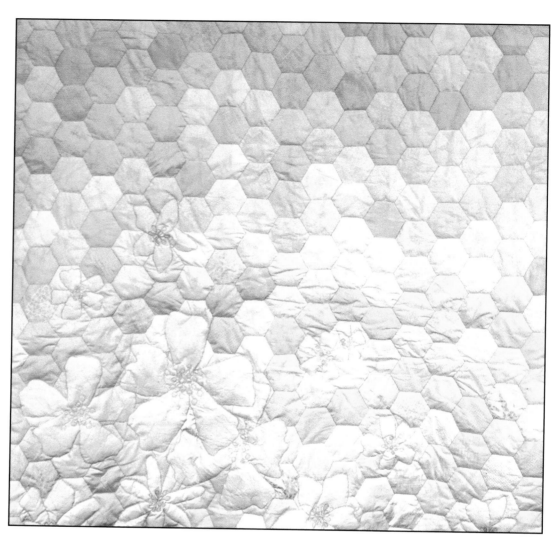

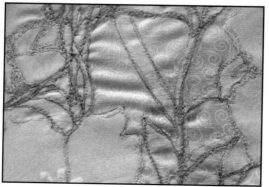

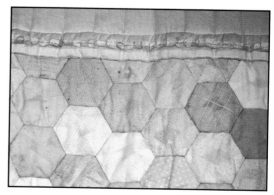

INSPIRATION

My love of Scotland grew from family holidays over the years, a love my grandmother shared. Participating in last year's grouse-hunting season at Dorback Estate gave time to draw inspirations from all around me, all of which I combined into a sketchbook of drawings, a collection of patchwork fabrics and a quilted bedspread in memory of my late grandmother. Rest in peace.

Alessandria Scarpari

San Giorgio di Mantova, Italy

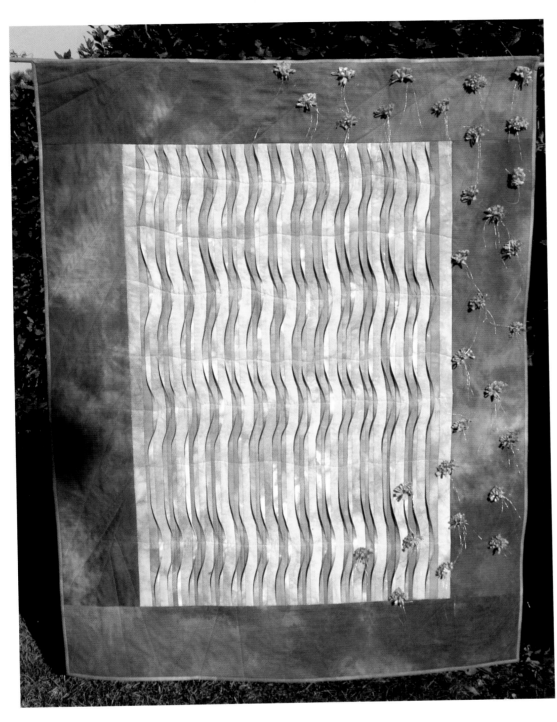

Emotional Thistles: The Colours of Friendship

57in (144cm) high, 43in (110cm) wide

Techniques

Made of 100% cotton fabric, hand-dyed using cold water Procion dyes – mixed to obtain purple and violet hues – machine pieced and machine quilted. The raw-edge thistles were made using a personal technique.

INSPIRATION

I love all types of quilts, but contemporary quilts are my favourite because they give me a sense of freedom when I make them. I particularly like playing with stripes – they are evocative of lines in the landscape and the effects of light on water – and I have represented both these elements in my quilt: the pleasing curves of the Lomondside hills, scattered with purple thistles to the edge of the shimmering waters of the loch. When I made this quilt I was remembering Scotland's beautiful scenery and my very special quilting friends that I visited in 2005.

Kimberly Robichaud Maine, USA

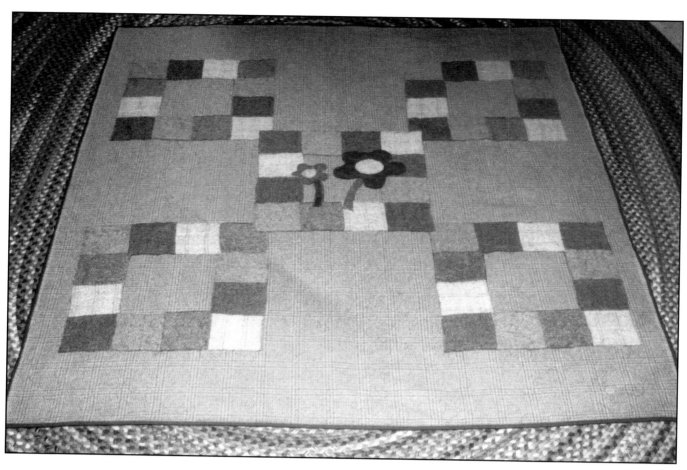

Embraced Growth

57in (145cm) high, 68in (173cm) wide

Techniques

Machine piecing, appliqué and quilting; binding finished by hand. Made from assorted wools from local woolen mills, reclaimed from my mother's clothes-making endeavours.

INSPIRATION

My sister introduced my family to a mystical and foggy Scotland on her wedding day to a Scottish musician. Our family now stretches from Maine to Scotland and has grown considerably; this quilt pattern celebrates the original five members of our family and the much-embraced growth. The fabrics commemorate the rich tradition of woolen mills in Maine, while the tweeds and plaids pay homage to Scotland's own gorgeous cloth heritage. The whimsical flowers are a nod to the fairy-tale impression Loch Lomond imprinted on all our memories forever.

San Antonio, Italy # Silvia Boiani

Star in the Loch

32in (82cm) square

Techniques

Made using Cindi Edgerton's Feathered Star pattern from her Little Bits series. Hand-dyed 100% cotton fabrics (Procion cold-water dyes): paper pieced and machine quilted.

INSPIRATION

I like to make traditional quilts. They make me feel happy and give me a sense of comfort: they also suit the style of my home. Paper piecing is one of my favourite techniques, and it's the best way of getting my points to meet. In my

Star in the Loch quilt I represent the light of a thousand winter stars, captured in the deep waters of the loch and then released to sparkle brilliantly across the surface of the loch, in the warmth of a summer's day.

Carol Villecco New Jersey, USA

My Highland Cathedral Window

58in (147cm) high, 37in (94cm) wide

Techniques

Cathedral Window blocks using a technique from *Machine-Stitched Cathedral Windows* by Shelly Swanland (Martingale & Co, 1999)

INSPIRATION

During my first visit to Scotland last September, two purchases and a surprise discovery in a church combined to inspire this quilt: the book *Cathedral Window Quilts* by Lynn Edwards, and *Highland Cathedral* on the Red Hot Chilli Pipers' CD *Bagrock to the Masses*. The largest pane in the quilt window is a photo of the Dunlop Badge from a window at Glasgow Cathedral; I am Scottish from my mother's side of the family – Dunlops and Stewarts.

Lichfield, Staffordshire # Steve Woodward

Log Cabin
60in (152cm) high,
72in (183cm) wide

Techniques
Fast-pieced Log Cabin, machine quilted. Made in silk, with cotton wadding and backing.

INSPIRATION

I discovered patchwork and quilting during my last year at Edinburgh University. I was asked by Ruth, Patricia and Isabel if I would go to Sweden to collect some Old Swedish Quilts from Asa Wettre's collection for an exhibition at the 2006 Loch Lomond Quilt Show. A free trip to Sweden, a few days' camping, then collect the quilts and back on the ferry to the UK – my dissertation was in and my exams finished, so it sounded great.

When I arrived with a friend in Gothenburg we decided to introduce ourselves to Asa before we headed of for a couple of nights' camping. The camping never happened as Asa insisted we stayed with her until it was time to take the quilts to Scotland. We slept in her work room at the top of her blue-and-white house with quilts all around. The colour and patterns in the old and new quilts were beautiful.

I helped at the Loch Lomond Quilt Show that year and saw all the quilts that I had brought over. The Log Cabin pattern was definitely my favourite, and I had some silk fabric that I had brought back from travels in Asia, so I decided to ask for a lesson in Log Cabin making. This is my first quilt, and reminds me of Scotland and travels to Sweden and Asia.

The Tartan Holdall Collection

THE enthusiastic and knowledgeable quilters of Region 16 of the Quilters' Guild of the British Isles can always be relied upon to rise to any challenge set them – whether that involves making a fantastic collection of journal quilts to raise money for the new Guild Museum in York; creating a beautiful banner for the Guild; or making a selection of small quilts for the Tartan Holdall Collection.

The brief was to create A3-sized quilts that would represent individual snapshots of Scotland past and present, the only other criterion being that they must contain a touch of tartan. The small quilts can be easily transported in a suitcase (or tartan holdall!), so that other Guilds and groups can enjoy the collection. The result is a true celebration of all things Scottish. As Lesley Hurrell, the Regional Co-ordinator says: 'It's great that we can reflect our country's quilting talent by putting together a collection of work by our very own Scottish Guild Members.'

And the talents of Scottish quilters were also used to create the banner (opposite). This was presented to the Quilters' Guild of the British Isles by Region 16 Scotland; it was designed by Gladys Williams and made, under her supervision, by sixteen members of the Sew 'n' Sews Quilt Group in Aberdeen. The banner was designed to reflect as many aspects of Scottish life as possible, many of which are famous the world over.

Side 1 is made up of four corner triangles featuring a castle, the Saltire, a black grouse and a distillery. The North Sea is represented by an oil rig with an approaching helicopter, the central oval consists of scenery and a golf course, whilst below the oval is Eilean Donan castle. Side 2 is also made up of four corner triangles consisting of deer, an eagle, a leaping salmon and highland cattle. The capital city is represented by Edinburgh Castle. The central oval shows scenery with the Glenfinnan Viaduct, local countryside and a typical Scottish village.

RIGHT: *Almost packed and ready to go! If you would like a visit from the Tartan Holdall Collection please contact: reg16@quiltersguild.org.uk*

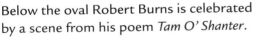

Below the oval Robert Burns is celebrated by a scene from his poem *Tam O' Shanter*.

Within the group there was a wide range of levels of quilting experience, and at times the learning curve was quite steep. The stitchers used many different techniques, and it was mostly left to the individual quilter to decide how best to construct her particular part of the project. Regular progress meetings were arranged and help was always on hand for people who felt they needed it.

Hanne, Ann Long and Helen also took on the challenge of putting all the pieces together. With so many people and different techniques involved this task was never going to be straightforward, but the skill of the stitchers overcame any challenges, and the different pieces have come together to create a spectacular finished result. The group is very proud that they were entrusted with this project, and are happy that it will be hanging at St Anthony's (the Quilters' Guild Museum in York) in the years to come.

The banner was made by the following quilters: Hanne Asbey; Mary Chesney; Barbara Downie; Catherine Fowler; Helen Hay; Maggie Ironside; Isobel Kennedy; Ann Lang; Ann Long; Norma Menzies; Sandra Reid; Joan Slade; Fay Smith; Ethel Taylor; Linda Taylor; Gladys Williams

The Tartan Holdall Collection

Hogmanay by Irene Turnbull

Bag Piper by Frances McArthur

Northern Lights by Bonnie McKerracher

Celtic Rose by Christine Blaikie

The Tartan Holdall Collection

Crazy Scots by Rachel Hawthorne

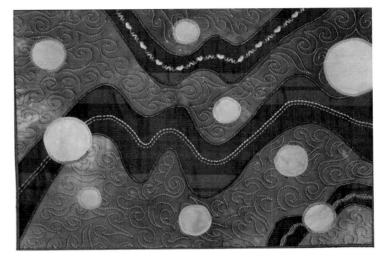

A Subtle Touch of Tartan by Georgina Chapman

This-tle Do Nicely by Catherine Pardoe

Happiness is Scottish Dancing by Sheila Chambers

The Tartan Holdall Collection

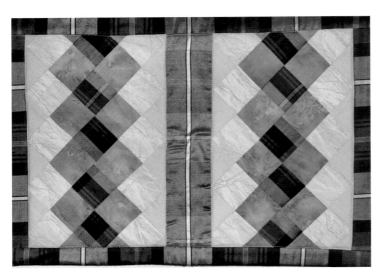

Scots in America by Muriel Gray

Dancing in the Midnight by Sheena Norquay

Eightsome Reel by Fiona Callander

Hearth, Heather and Hillside by Annette Bruton

The Tartan Holdall Collection

Autumn in Scotland by Liz Duke

Dreamscape by Sheila Robertson

Lindsay Tartan Glitz by Linzi Upton

Hector by Catriona Stirling

The Tartan Holdall Collection

High Summer by Christine Ireland

Flower of Scotland by Andrea Lee

Ben Lomond and Loch Lomond by Tanja Burlison

Fragments by Joyce Watson

The Tartan Holdall Collection

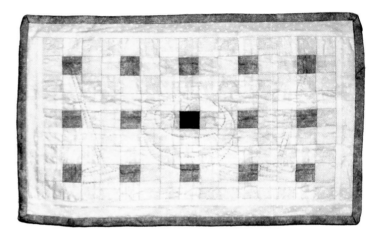

Happy Chappie by Sandra Shedden

A Touch of Tartan by Ann Hunter

A Touch of Tartan by Anne Haughs

Lilts and Kilts by Dorothy Polson Brown

The Tartan Holdall Collection

Lybster Harbour by Ann Cullop

A Wee Bit of Scotland Reaches Everywhere
by Carol Judge

Moonlit Brae by Lois Bowen

Home for Christmas by Marie MacLeod

The Tartan Holdall Collection

A Touch of Tartan by Margaret Morrow

The Home Coming 2009 by Isobel Campbell

Autumn to Winter by Lesley Hurrell

Follow the Arrow by Catriona Stirling

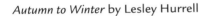

The Tartan Holdall Collection

Thistle by Morven Roche

Last Laugh by Anne Witcomb

Speed and Beauty by Joanne McCue

Land of My Heart Forever by Margaret Boe

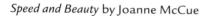

The Tartan Holdall Collection

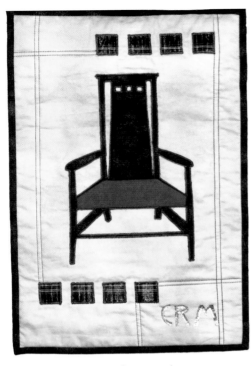

CRM by Lilian Loudoun

Tartan Toon by Catherine Waterson

A Touch of Tartan by Liz Ferguson

Celtic Wreath by Jean Macdonald

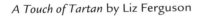

The Tartan Holdall Collection

Scottie Dog by Moira Rose

Highland Fling by Anne MacLean

Three Wee Craws by Liz Weston

To Honour Mackintosh by Margaret McGeever

The Tartan Holdall Collection

My Heart is in the Highlands by Mavis Mackie

Uisge Beatha (Water of Life) by Gillian McCallum

Portrait of the Poet by Patricia Freeth

Uisge Beatha (Water of Life) by Violet Tosh

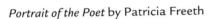

The Tartan Holdall Collection

Queen's Cross Church Glasgow
by Catherine Waterson

The Scottish Parliament Building, Holyrood
by Anne Hoggan

The Scottish Wanderer by Pauline Brown

Celtic Cross by Jessie Smart

The Tartan Holdall Collection

Thistle Symbol Quilt by Frieda Oxenham

My Hairdresser Wears Tartan Trousers
by Alison Jabs

Thistle While You Work by Mary Hall

Westering Home by Fran Bonetti

New Home Quilt
and the Oasis Group

RIGHT: *Many of the women brought their traditional sewing skills to the group project.*

BELOW: *The quilt on display in the Long Gallery of the Burrell.*

BELOW RIGHT: *Volunteers and Oasis members working together.*

SCOTLAND is a modern vibrant country, with individuals from many different people-groups making it their new home each year. For the past two years Ruth has worked with the Maryhill Integration Network in the North of Glasgow. MIN is a charity that was formed in 2001 to support refugees and immigrants to the city; Ruth has worked with the women's group Oasis. Both of the two main projects she has been involved with have enabled the women to take part in the 16 Days of Action Against Gender Violence. Many of the refugee women have themselves suffered horrendous violence; for many this is their reason for seeking refuge in Scotland.

In 2008 Ruth worked with the group in October and November to make a quilt to hang in their new headquarters in Maryhill. The quilt would also be displayed as part of the events organised by Maryhill during the 16 Days of Action. Poetry, drama, dance and an international fashion show were all ingredients in their events.

The group is made up of regular and occasional attendees, of young and old, of mothers and grandmothers, of women from Europe, the old Soviet bloc, Africa, Asia and South America – the sheer number of languages spoken can confound the visitor. Teaching is mainly done by demonstration – and definitely couldn't be done without the help of many volunteers.

LEFT: *The finished quilt.*

BELOW: *One of the posters for the Days of Action featured the quilt as part of the backdrop.*

BOTTOM: *The quilt comes together ...*

The group members had visited the Burrell Museum earlier in the year and been inspired by the temporary exhibition of the Museum's collection of *suzani* hangings. It was decided that the quilt would reflect the spirit of the *suzani* work.

In the limited time available it was not possible to recreate the embroideries using traditional methods, so Ruth took a little liberty in introducing everyone to the joys of bonding web (see page 62). The quilt was made up of 12 blocks, with each block being the work of several people. Borders, wadding and backing were added to complete the project. The purple borders remind us of the hard-fought battle for women's suffrage.

The *suzanis* are filled with stylized flowers which flow across the designs. So using plain-coloured quilting fabrics, large and small flowers were cut our and positioned in the blocks. The flowers seemed a good metaphor for the lives that women lead: some live in the sun and are blessed with long and happy lives, others survive in spite of poor soil, terrible weather and

being trampled underfoot. Members of the group produced some fantasy flowers, flowers that reminded them of home, and a few stylized Scottish flowers – the thistle and the bluebell/harebell.

The quilt shows a huge range of skill levels, ideas and colours, but at the same time the finished hanging works as a whole – it has become much more than the sum of its parts and has been displayed at various venues around the Glasgow area.

Inspired by the Burrell

BELOW: A sketchbook page showing paper cutouts inspired by the suzani hangings

The Burrell collection is one of Scotland's jewels. The modern museum building, in Pollock Park, houses the wonderful, eclectic collection of Sir William Burrell. Although this was given to the people of Glasgow in 1944, it wasn't until 1983 that the museum opened. With a collection of over 9,000 articles, from armour to tapestries, Chinese vases to stained glass windows, of course not all the collection can be on display at any one time.

The museum has a small but important collection of *suzani* embroideries that were bought by Burrell in 1925. The hangings were originally from Khanate of Bukhara, now the Republic of Uzbekistan. The hangings are not on permanent display in the Burrell – their glorious colours and silk thread need to be protected from light and moisture – but

they were on show from summer 2008 until January 2009. This was an exhibition that attracted many visitors who were 'stunned by the colours' and 'delighted to see them on display,' to judge by the comments in the visitors books.

An Iranian Farsi word, *suzani* means 'needle.' The hangings were a domestic craft, made to cover doorways, tables, cradles and the wedding bed. In each community a *Kalamkash* or draughtswoman would preserve the traditional patterns and designs. She would be paid to draw out a design for whatever was needed; the designs were then cut up and distributed to various family members who embroidered over the marked patterns. The *Kalamkash* drew the patterns with only a few tools – a marking pen and bowls or plates – adding her own touches as well as the traditional shapes.

To those who know their quilt history, this sounds so familiar. From the professional quilt markers or stampers in Wales and the Northeast of England, to the designers of Baltimore blocks in 19th century America, domestic textile crafts have developed in very similar ways. Despite their exotic appearance the actual flower and leaf shapes can also be found in Welsh and North Country quilting patterns, as well as in appliqué quilts. It's probably hardly surprising that flower shapes echo each other around the world, or that a central area is surrounded by borders. At the same time these hangings seem wonderfully different and surprisingly familiar – a domestic craft lifted to an art form by the women who stitched it.

The Oasis Women's group quilt has inspired a few cushions and a small wall-hanging using the same plain-coloured cotton fabrics bonded onto a neutral background, embellished with simple embroidery stitches used alongside some traditional hand quilting. The stylised

flower and stem shapes were cut freehand into folded circles of greaseproof paper. This method was developed from the same technique as taught by Lilian Hedley in her *Design a North Country Quilt* class.

Mighty Oaks

THE OAK TREE has been held in high esteem by many cultures in Europe. Being amongst the tallest and oldest of living things, the oak was foremost amongst venerated trees and was associated with gods who had power over rain, thunder and lightning. Ancient kings wore crowns of oak leaves to symbolize the god they represented on earth, and the 'Corona Civica,' a civic crown of oak leaves, was presented to Roman soldiers who had saved the life of a fellow soldier in battle.

The ancient Celts worshipped in oak groves, and in Britain many early Christian churches and monasteries were built over such sites using timber from the groves. It is said that St Columba had a great love and respect for oak trees; he avoided felling them whenever possible, but did build a chapel on the island of Iona using timber from the great oak woods on nearby Mull.

In pagan cultures the oak is sacred to the waxing year, and the Oak King is worshipped at the Summer Solstice. Oak wood is still burned at the May 1st fires of Beltane and at the Midwinter Solstice celebrations, and several specifically-named oaks feature in folklore and history throughout the country. Oak leaves were pinned to the plaids and bonnets of those who fought for Bonnie Prince Charlie in the Jacobite uprising of 1745, and oak leaves remain a meaningful symbol for the Royal Clan Stewart.

During the Industrial Revolution oak bark was valued for its high tannin content, and large amounts were sent from managed oak woodlands in the north west of Scotland to Glasgow, to be used in the leather-tanning process. The bark and acorns yield a blackish-brown dye, and oak galls give a strong black dye which was used in the production of ink. Many woods in Argyll and the surrounding areas were coppiced for charcoal-making for the iron-smelting industry. These historic woods were well managed and can still be seen today. The loch-side and islands of Loch Lomond are rich in pendunculate and sessile oaks[1], which are dispersed amongst ash, elder and alder to form a rich mosaic of tree and plant life.

Leaf patterns are common to all quilting. Used mainly in appliqué, the unmistakable shape of an oak leaf and acorn are shown diagrammatically as stitching and filling patterns in Averil Colby's book *Quilting*[2], where they feature

[1] Pendunculate oak – acorn has long stem. Sessile oak – acorn grows directly on the main stem. Leaf shape and length differ slightly.

[2] Averil Colby, *Quilting*, BT Batsford Ltd, p131/132,

in a gallery of leaf shapes that were worked into Welsh quilts, quilts of South England, and North Country quilts.

LOMOND OAKS

The oak leaf used in *Lomond Oaks* owes much to a diagram in Colby's book, taken from a motif of quilted oak leaves on 'a black silk dress made in Devonshire, 1868.' The 19th-century leaf motif has been slightly modified and stylized, and alternate leaf shapes have been flipped on the vertical axis and nudged together to create a 'running leaf' pattern that imitates the oaks that line the banks of Loch Lomond. The central leaf rib has been straightened to form a continuous zigzag that contrasts quite sharply with the curvilinear outline and gently arched veins of the leaf. When set together the columns of running leaf patterns make diamond-like shapes. The stitch pattern has been worked with backstitch in a white-on-white wholecloth quilting style, to create a 25in square bed cushion.

INCHAILLOCH

Inchailloch is one of Loch Lomond's sixty or so islands and islets; it lies a short ferryboat ride away from the village of Balmaha, on the east side of Loch Lomond. The island is cloaked in oak woodland. In the hooped work, two slightly different oak leaf shapes and sizes

and a short-stemmed sessile acorn template have been arranged to form an 'island of oak' that is worked in large quilting stitches, using dark green silk thread on a light green linen/cotton mix fabric. *Lomond Oaks* and *Inchcailloch* were designed and made in celebration of the magnificent oaks of Scotland.

ABOVE: *White cushion on Patricia's bed, quilted with a wholecloth oakleaf design* Lomond Oaks. *The green quilt on the bed was made by Makepeace Quilters as a surprise gift for her 60th birthday.*

LEFT: *The original oak leaf design by Patricia*

FAR LEFT: *Hand stitching a cushion with the design*

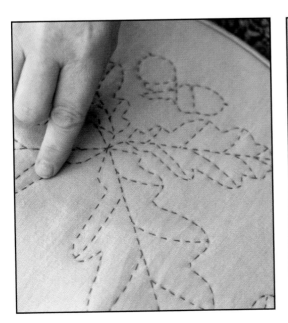

Gone Fishing

YOU are never far from water in Scotland. Thousands of miles of mainland and island coastline, and a patchwork of rivers, streams, burns and lochs – most of them home to fish of some kind – means that fish have a significant part in Scotland's art, literature, industry and food.

The City of Glasgow's coat of arms includes a leaping salmon with a ring in its mouth: a ring given by King Redderech to his fickle wife Queen Languoreth, who in turn gave it to a handsome soldier. When the King caught up with the soldier, who was sleeping by a river, he took the ring and threw it into the water, where it was swallowed by a salmon. When Redderech insisted that his Queen produce the ring, she was saved by St Mungo who miraculously caught the salmon and recovered the ring.

St Mungo founded an educational community in the 6th century on the site of what is now Glasgow cathedral: the City of Glasgow was born. The modern city's motto is 'Let Glasgow Flourish', a shortened version of St Mungo's original, 'Let Glasgow Flourish By The Preaching Of The Word.' The medieval city seal shows St Mungo with the salmon hanging from his ear.

The migratory Atlantic Salmon (Salmo salar) is found in Scotland's seventy-five salmon-fishing rivers, from the Borders to the Highlands – the birthplace of salmon fly-fishing. Having run the gauntlet of killer whales, dolphins and seals during an epic salt-water journey of thousands of miles – from perhaps as far as the Davis Strait on the west coast of Greenland – across the Atlantic Ocean and through the North Sea, the salmon return. Having found their way, guided possibly by stars, local differences in the earth's magnetic field, ocean currents, chemical memory, or an irrepressible and unfathomable internal geography, the fish make their way up fresh-water rivers and falls, usually returning to the clean sparkling water of their birth, their home pools in the Scottish mountains. There, in quieter shallows, the salmon spawns and another cycle in the endless course of river life begins.

The salmon is characterised by its resolve, its striving, and a muscular shining body that drives hard, making spectacular leaps through fast-flowing and freely-tumbling waters. The fish makes an excellent subject for a small wall-hanging, the centre or border panels of a fly-fisherman's quilt, or a treasured fireside cushion.

In **King of the River**, salmon and water leap from layered, hand-dyed cotton organza –

King of the River

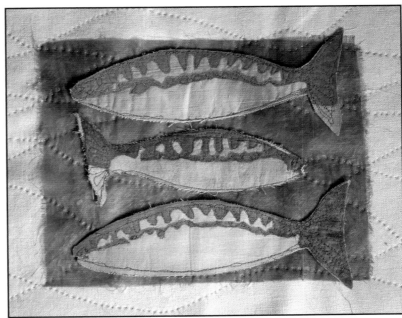

small remnants from a previous quilting project, buried at the bottom of a stash. They were machined with a variegated-colour thread, using a short-length straight stitch, then framed with a two-strip border at the top and bottom of the panel, and livened with single chain stitches worked randomly in white crochet cotton on the lower half of the picture and around the body of the fish, to echo the droplet motif in the border batik. The 19½in x 12½in panel imitates more 'spirit of salmon' than accurate salmon anatomy, but cloth and stitch work together to capture the power of both fish and water.

The fishy theme continues in *Gone Fishing* (above). Bobbing on the water, a line out from the back of the dinghy ... the easiest ever way to catch fish. Within minutes, the line is heavy with dozens of distinctively-pattern mackerel that have made their way to you. Memories of freshly-caught fish cooked over a wood fire on the beach, cold beer, and stories that grow taller as the sun sinks lower. Hand-dyed cotton and silk organdie were layered, free-machined and cut away to create the fish; the dancing sea is made from silk organdie, layered over silk tops and linen and hand-stitched with ripples. A happy memory committed to cloth.

ABOVE LEFT: *Ruth's sketchbook* – Gone Fishing

ABOVE: *Journal quilt – inspired by a day of mackerel fishing*

Dancing Thistle

RIGHT: Dancing
Thistle *quilt*

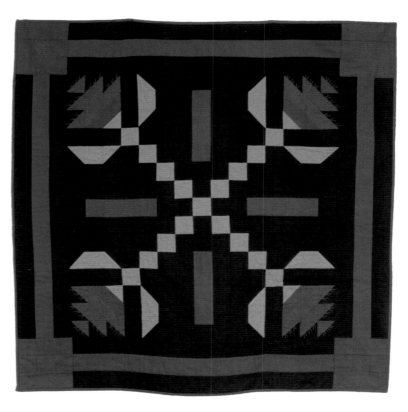

'In Scotland grows a
warlike flower,
Too rough to bloom
in lady's bower'
wrote the Scottish
poet Allan
Cunningham in *The
Thistle's Grown Aboon
the Rose*, a not-too-
subtle comment on the
relationship between
the Scots and the
English.

The thistle has been a
special emblem for
Scotland since the time
of King James III (1460
-1488), when it was
first used as a royal
symbol on silver coins.
According to one
legend, the thistle
protected clansmen
from a party of Norse invaders who
had removed their footwear for a silent
attack on a Scottish encampment. The
barefoot raiders walked into patch of
thistles and their cries woke the
sleeping men who were able to beat the
attackers off. The thistle was hailed as
a protector of the people and it has
become the national flower of
Scotland. Thistles decorate Scotland's
highest order of chivalry, the Order of
the Thistle, and are incorporated into
Scotland's version of the Royal Coat of
Arms of the United Kingdom, where
several flowers sit jauntily above the
Latin motto *Nemo me impune lacessit*,
usually translated as 'No-one provokes
me with impunity.'

When the thistle opens, its prickly body
is crowned with a beautiful rose-purple
inflorescence, a composite flower made
up of many tiny flowers which, says
Cunningham in his poem, '*Bright like a
steadfast star... smiles.*' Bees hurry to its
nectar and birds to its seeds. Straight

and proud, sinuous or softly rounded,
the thistle flower-head and leaves are
constantly being reinterpreted for use in
jewellery, stained glass, textiles, ceramics
and company logos.

The motif can be seen in the 1920s and
1930s quilts made by members of church
guilds in the Scottish Borders town of
Hawick. The Hawick 'heart and thistle'
motif distinguishes the quilts from their
Welsh and North Country cousins. The
shape is distinctive and simple, and the
Dancing Thistle block is based on the
same principles.

The motif has been reduced to a basic
geometric form, and the quilt in the main
picture has been made using bold jewel-
coloured and black fabrics. The blocks
are constructed from 2in squares/half-
square triangles, and the thistle motif is
set on the diagonal. This arrangement
allows the barbed plant stems to flow
across the centre of the quilt, creating
strong movement and making a textile

'drawing' reminiscent of weapons laid out for a Highland sword dance – appropriate for Cunningham's 'warlike flower.' A less prickly, more friendly and uncomplicated leaf shape emphasizes the upward lines of the plant's aspect, and fancifully imitates the upheld arms of an invisible sword dancer.

The sashing is set with colours used in the flower-head: this breaks up the expanse of black and helps to pull the design elements together. An easy border, corner blocks and coloured binding complete the design. Three parallel lines of outline quilting emphasize the thistle motifs and help to soften the grid-lines of the blocks. The finished quilt measures 42in (106cm) square. The thistle stalks and leaves are worked with an irregular seed stitch using a colour-matched coton à broder: extra-large fly stitches grouped in threes emphasize the posture of the flower-head. The embellishment gives texture and depth to the motif, and the outcome is vibrant and lively. The block is adaptable: nine blocks could be set on point and alternated with a plain block to make a larger quilt, and a single block makes an attractive cushion front.

A very different thistle emerges with the use of soft colours, muted prints and/or plains. They evoke the quiet of a misty

Scottish glen, and the softness of popular names for the Scotch Thistle – cotton thistle, woolly thistle – and the thistledown that lifts and drifts on autumn winds. When worked in silks or other luxury fabrics the thistle manifests a regal appearance, in keeping with its honoured place on coinage and in heraldry.

The thistle block, designed by Patricia, used on its own in a silk cushion

An alternative colourway sample of the block

Eilean Air An Oir
Cuibhrigean Eilean Leodhais

THE QUILTMAKERS

Rosslyn Barton
Calmac Ferry 'Isle of Lewis' (11)
Church (14)

Frances Caple
Black House (7)
Beach (15)

Cath Dodd
Sheep (17)

Pam Lye
Oystercatcher (6)
Butt of Lewis Lighthouse (19)

Lilian Maclennan
Uig Chessman (5)
Sgoth – fishing boat (10)
Leverhulme Bridge (18)

Roseann Macleod
Herring (12);
Spinning Wheel (16)

Christine MacRae
Callanish Stones (3);
Thistles (13)

Ishbal Scott
Lews Castle (2)
Water Lily (8)
The Orb (Harris Tweed Trademark) (20)

Anne Williamson
Map of Isle of Lewis (1)
Eagle (4)

The quilt is on permanent display at Stornoway Airport, welcoming visitors to Lewis

EILEAN AIR AN OIR (or *Island on the Edge*) was made by the Isle of Lewis Stornoway-based quilting group Cuibhrigean Eilean Leodhais; they created it for the 2007 Loch Lomond Quilt Show's 'Far & Away' competition, which invited participants to take their inspiration from Scotland's islands and island communities. Nine quilters chose to make a group entry using the Harris Tweed still produced on the island.

The timing was difficult: the remaining large manufacturer of tweed had just changed hands, and the community was in a heated debate on a proposal to build a wind farm on the island. In the unsettled atmosphere, it seemed right to the quilters

Thermador wadding and a purple toning cotton backing made up the three layers of the quilt. Coton perlé and variegated cotton thread were used for machine quilting, and the plain border was hand-quilted with a rope design that reflected the island's fishing heritage.

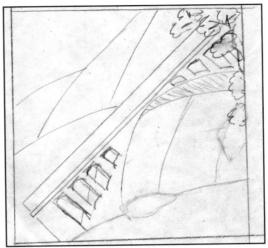

DRAWING: BRIDGE BLOCK

'Bridge to Nowhere,' built by Lord Leverhulme in 1920. Picture built up and ironed onto stabilizer: zig-zagged using smoke-coloured filament. Bridge and rocks superimposed and appliquéd on. A variety of crocheted textured threads used for trees.

that their quilt should reflect what was important to them in the landscape, traditions and history of the island. Lewis is known in Gaelic as *Eilean an Fhraoich*, the 'Heather Isle,' so a purple-heathery check tweed was chosen as the focus, together with plain tweeds in colours drawn from the check. Plain blocks would alternate with pictorial blocks, and all blocks would be set on point. There was a setback when the quilters discovered that the mill had unexpectedly run out of stock and they had to wait for more tweed to be woven in time for the competition.

The quilters worked on 9in blocks – each block depicting a landscape or an object of personal significance – and chose the techniques with which they would interpret their block. Over the weeks the group learned new skills and learned to work together, sharing both knowledge and materials in what they described as 'an infinitely pleasurable experience.'

Some of the group were experienced in working with Harris Tweed, which was cut on the cross and stabilized to preserve the bias edges. Balancing the colours of the blocks and matching the lines of the checks in the alternating blocks proved extremely challenging.

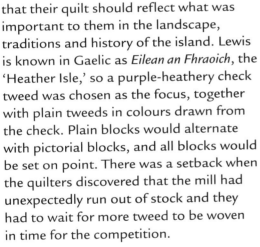

ORIGINAL DRAWING.

DRAWING: CALLANISH STONES BLOCK

Iconic site. Finding correct tweed colour for stones difficult: darker tweed used for shadow. Stones zigzag-appliquéd with invisible thread: sky hand quilted with silver lurex and silk tops: stone beads and mixed fibre yarn in foreground.

WORKING THE SPINNING WHEEL BLOCK

An extremely delicate cutting-out and bonding of tweed on tweed process. Wheel outline stitched with invisible thread; details stitched in black. A fine zigzag stitch in gold metallic thread forms the wool that winds around the spinning wheel.

Inspired by Harris Tweed

Harris Tweed is made by islanders on Harris, Lewis, Uist and Barra, using virgin wool that has been dyed and spun in the Outer Hebrides. It is known for its hard-wearing properties, which have made it very suitable for outdoor clothing. The subtle colours now come from a mixture of natural and commercial dyes.

RIGHT: Harris, a heavyweight quilt made for Alistair by Patricia in 2002, from a variety of hand-loomed tweeds. These include Harris Tweeds gifted by a friend whose family croft once had its own weaving shed and loom, and a soft herringbone tweed made in the Aberdeen district. All the colours of the tweeds are brought together in four diamonds of needlecord which features autumnal organic forms and a black ground. Machine pieced, and backed with a soft, dark brown cotton bought on a visit to Carrefour du Patchwork, Alsace. The two-layer quilt is machine quilted, and has a Harris tweed binding; it's 'buttoned' with pieces of wood and horn.

Tweed originated in the borders of Scotland and was originally spelt tweel, but thanks to the popularity of the novels of Sir Walter Scott and a clerk who copied tweel as tweed, the spelling changed.

Writing in 1988 in *Traditional Crafts of Scotland*, Jenny Carter and Janet Rae record the work of Marion Campbell, who then was in her seventies. Her wool comes from the adjoining croft and is coloured with natural dyes from the local lichens, 'yellow flowers, iris roots (which yield yellow and brown), or with chemical dyes for the greens and blues.' (page 35) In this book other traditions such as 'waulking' the cloth are recorded.

'Waulking' was at one time a social occasion, with neighbours joining the weaver as the cloth was cut from the loom and further finished by pulling, rubbing and soaking in ammonia. The effect is to firm and shrink the woven fabric to its finished width of only 29 inches. Harris Tweed always bears the trade mark orb (see pages 6 and 52), usually with the name of the island it was made on underneath.

These two quilts were made as gifts for men, and it seemed appropriate to use Harris Tweed – long a favourite fabric for men's jackets. The quilts were made from a mixture of used (recycled from old jackets) and new tweed. *In Rod We Trust* was inspired by Rod's own love of Harris Tweed. Simple piecing and firm stitching were all that was needed to make the most of the texture and colours of the tweed. The quilt is layered with cotton wadding and backing, and finished with a binding of tartan.

In Rod We Trust,
*a traditional British
Strippy quilt made as a
thank you by Ruth,
Patricia and Isabel for
their good friend Rod
Hannah.*

Lines Across Scotland

ABOVE: *Three tweed and boutis cushions, made by Patricia Macindoe. Left* Lomond Light, *centre* Cup and Ring, *right* Celtic Knot.

BACKGROUND QUILT: *2009 Raffle Quilt for Comfort Quilts*

(www.comfortquilts.co.uk)

MYSTERY surrounds the linear 'cup and ring' rock carvings (petroglyphs) found on natural rock outcrops, boulders and megaliths in Scotland. Some carvings are near to – or are part of – cairns and burial mounds, and the symbols may have significance for burial practices and beliefs about ancestors and afterlife. Carvings are also found on standing stones and in stone circles, and may indicate a religious and ritualistic meaning. Others occur on rock outcrops that give an uninterrupted view over the surrounding country.

The purpose and meaning of the cup and ring carvings is not understood, but their elegant simplicity of form is easily appreciated. Like those found in northern England and in other countries around the world, the carvings are thought to be prehistoric, being estimated at 4000-5000 years old and belonging to the Neolithic and Bronze Ages. The circular hollows and surrounding rings occur singly or as multiples, and sometimes have a gutter which leads out from the hollow in the middle, which may suggest the possibility of use beyond symbolism? Modern re-creations of the cup and ring, made by archaeologists using a deer antler to peck the symbol into rock, have shown how well the marks stand out from the darker weathered stone surface when they are first carved. Clearly the carvings were made to be seen.

The *Cup and Ring, Celtic Knot* and *Lomond Light* designs have all been worked in the boutis techniques of Bas-Languedoc, France. In 'piqûre de Marseille' style, tiny 'point de piqûre' (backstitches) have been worked on traditional white Batiste cloth, to make sylph-like outlining forms. The small window panel (front cover, middle row, left) allows light to pass through the worked centre panel, and demonstrates the fine translucent quality of boutis work. Juxtaposed with tweed in the cushions, the boutis sits like snow capping a stone wall: the delicate and the strong brought harmoniously together.

CELTIC KNOT

Unbroken line and interlaced knot patterns are found in 3rd- and 4th-century Roman floor mosaics and architecture, and in book illuminations of Byzantine, Islamic, Coptic, Medieval Russian, Ethiopian, European and Celtic traditions. In Scotland, Celtic knots can be seen on Christian monuments, especially 'high crosses' – free-standing Christian crosses made of stone. The crosses usually feature a ring surrounding the intersection of the vertical and horizontal parts of the monument, and the knots may be interlaced with spirals, key patterns, human and entwined zoomorphic designs.

Two of the most well-known and beautifully-ornamented manuscripts that incorporate Celtic design are the 8th Century *Book of Kells* (thought to have been made at a monastery on the island of Iona in honour of St Columba), and the *Lindisfarne Gospels* (the illuminated Latin manuscript made in Lindisfarne, Northumbria, and now in the British Library in London).

ABOVE: Celtic Knot *cushion*
BELOW: Lomond Light *cushion*

LOMOND LIGHT

Loch Lomond Youth Hostel is a grand 19th-century country house, a 'towered and turreted extravaganza of Scottish Baronial architecture' set in beautiful wooded parkland overlooking Loch Lomond. Built in the 1860s for a wealthy Glasgow merchant, it was bequeathed to the government, who in turn gave it to the Scottish Youth Hostel Association. The building maintains many of its original decorative features, including stained glass windows. The play of light through simple lead and glass leaf-like shapes was the inspiration for the design, resolved in a boutis and Harris Tweed cushion and given to celebrate the wedding anniversary of very dear friends. The dissecting lines create a grid reminiscent of shapes found in the furniture and architecture of Scotland's Charles Rennie Mackintosh.

Nessie: the legend and the truth

ABOVE: *The rocky shore of Loch Ness*

LEGEND has long held that Loch Ness hides a wonderful secret: an animal left from a time before man. A crypto-zoological puzzle; perhaps Nessie is a plesiosaurus or a zeuglodon? (Not words often mentioned in quilting books.) Loch Ness is 23 miles long and 745 feet deep, and the second-largest body of water in Scotland; only Loch Lomond is larger. With many remote beaches and small inlets, there are many places for a legend to hide.

Sea, loch and river myths abound in Scotland. Selkie are seal-like creatures that shed their seal skins to walk on land as beautiful young women. If a man finds the shed skin he can force the Selkie to stay as his wife. But a man silly enough to be tempted into the water by these beauties will not be seen again. Male Selkie are responsible for storms and the capsizing of boats.

Kelpies are the water goblins who take the form of horses on land. When a weary traveller tries to ride the horse, the Kelpie/horse dives into the water,

drowning the poor victim. Shellycoats are a form of bogeymen that live in rivers; they are covered in shells which rattle as they move. Somehow these myths seemed a little unbelievable to us and certainly not suitable for a young child's quilt; so, back to our beloved Nessie.

The truth about Nessie is ... that we all hope the legend is true and that she's alive and well living in Loch Ness. In this quilt she's doing even better than that: Nessie has found love and fulfilment in motherhood. Niall, Nelina, Nicol and Nula are the naughtiest, nosiest and nippiest wee ones you could hope to find in any loch. Easier to spot than Nessie because of their juvenile colours, they won't get their adult colours until they're at least half way to becoming a full-grown myth. And yet at the same time they're harder to spot because of their sheer speed; some people may have caught a glimpse out of the corners of their eyes, but little Nessies are always gone by the time anyone can turn to get a proper look.

MAKING NESSIE

Our quilt is 26 x 33in – a useful size for a cot, car or playmat quilt for a young child. First of all we found a 'water' fabric; most medium- to light-coloured blue/green pattered fabrics will work for this. Green fabrics – leaf patterned or striped – work for the reedy border. Nessie herself looks good in a batik print – the colour choice is up to you. The same for her babies – do remember that young animals often have a different look to the adults. We added a subtle touch of tartan for her neck, body and tail frills. Why not add your own tartan; if you don't have one – borrow one.

We used an iron on bonding web* on the green fabric and the Nessie and baby Nessie fabrics. A light iron-on adhesive like this helps to position and stabilize the fabrics, which are then easy to secure with stitching. A useful tip: make a small 'quilt sandwich' using a spare piece of top fabric with a shape bonded to it, layered with your chosen wadding and backing. Try out some of your machine's stitches to outline the shape – experiment with zigzags in a variety of sizes, buttonhole stitch and other decorative stitches to see which suits your Nessie the best.

*See tips for using iron-on adhesive sheets in the 'how to get started' section on page 62.

ABOVE: *The Nessie quilt*

LEFT: *You are never far away from water in Scotland – so it isn't surprising that there are so many mysterious water myths!*

Be Inspired!

FAR RIGHT: *Detail from Ruth's dye recipe book*
RIGHT: *an inspirational sketchbook*
BELOW: *Part of the Winter section of* Four Seasons in Log Cabin, *using hand dyed fabrics, antique ribbons, buttons and beads, and* The Blues Don't Bother Me. *Both quilts by Ruth.*

Patchwork and quilting is for all people who love to stitch. For anyone who loves to create using colour and texture. For everyone who loves to work with their hands. It can be taken to extraordinary levels of craftsmanship, but at the same time it can be thoroughly enjoyed by a beginner.

Patchwork and quilting now covers a huge range of techniques; from traditional to contemporary; from hand stitching to computer-aided long-arm machines; from recycled, almost no-cost, options to the limits of your bank account (and beyond!) The journeys that you can take are almost limitless.

If you are one of those people who just loves to dive in – go ahead: jump! But if you need to take things in a more considered way, why don't you choose a starting-point, focusing on what you like doing? Be inspired by what's around you: for instance, take the colours of your favourite beach photograph, and use them to make a Log Cabin bed quilt, or test out some fabrics or techniques on a cushion or wall-hanging. Adapt the swirling lines of the waves' edges to create a wonderful quilting pattern, or use the contrasting textures of the sea and the sand to inspire unusual fabric choices.

Find a friend (or several) who also would like to take their patchwork and quilting in new directions, and work together, setting small challenges and keeping to a timetable. Join a design class, or start exploring the City & Guilds route, and before you know it a star will be born!

Patchwork and Quilting Tips
How to get started

THESE two pages come with a short warning: patchwork and quilting is highly addictive – proceed at your own risk.

To go into a patchwork and quilting shop can be both a total delight and total sensory overload. Rows of wonderful fabric, inspiring books, and gadgets that promise all your points will point and your edges be perfectly straight – but what do you really need to start with? Well, you will definitely need some fabric, but our guess is that if you are reading this book you already have some fabric – a 'stash' of material that you've probably collected over a number of years. You'll also need a basic sewing kit of needles, thread, pins and cutting equipment (scissors, and possibly a rotary cutter and associated tools – an 'unpicker' is also very handy … !) Let's have a quick look at each of these items.

• Fabric
100% cottons are ideal, and much easier to start with than velvets and silks. Why don't you sort out two or three that look good together – but perhaps not your all-time favourite special fabric? Recycle some old pyjamas or lightweight furnishing fabrics for your first try.

• Needles
For hand piecing a medium-sized fine needle works well; the higher the number of the needle size, the bigger it is. If you're going to be sewing 100% cotton fabric try and source 100% cotton thread; good-quality thread makes sewing more of a pleasure.

• Pins
Try and find some fine pins – big pins make big holes!

• Cutting equipment
You'll need a fine pair of scissors and a larger pair of scissors – sharp is always better than blunt. In addition, most

ABOVE: *Traditional fabrics and sewing tools*

quilters now cut out their pieces using a rotary cutter: once you get the hang of them, they give you a fast accurate cut. To use a rotary cutter you will also need a quilters' ruler and a self-healing cutting mat. There are so many different-sized rulers: a good ruler to start with is one which measures 24in long by 6in wide. An A2-sized cutting mat is not too large or too small. Remember that the mat needs to be kept in a flat position, and away from heat.

Should you stitch by hand or machine? There is no right or wrong when it comes to choosing whether to hand or machine stitch a quilt. Chose whatever method suits you: both have pros and cons, and there are some techniques which you can only do with machine stitching and vice versa.

Patchwork and Quilting Tips *continued*

RIGHT: *Rotary cutter, quilters' ruler and cutting mat – the equipment of today's quilters.*

What kind of machine? The simple answer is: one that works! This remark isn't as flippant as it sounds; a machine in good working order, that is easy to load a bobbin into and easy to thread, is much less frustrating than one on which the tension is constantly slipping etc. So, old or new, make sure you take care of the machine you have. A machine that does straight stitches, can reverse a few stitches, has a zigzag stitch (and maybe a few other ones), and on which you can drop the feed dogs. If you're buying a machine, ask if the model you are looking at can be supplied with a ¼in foot, a free machining foot and a walking foot. If these sound like double Dutch, they won't after a little more exposure to the quilting sorority.

TOP TIP: join a quilting group. Quilting is much more fun, and easier to learn, with fellow enthusiasts. Look in your local library or put a card up in the local shop or supermarket – try your local Guild or the Quilters' Guild of the British Isles (see contact details on p63). Good friendships and great quilts are made with help and support. Quilters are the most sharing, open and generous group of people you could hope to meet.

If you really can't go to a group, the next best is probably a good book – our two all-time favourites are *The Art of Classic Quiltmaking* by Harriet Hargrave and Sharyn Craig, and *The Complete Book of Patchwork, Quilting and Appliqué* by Linda Seward. In both machine and hand methods are clearly and accurately described.

Tips for using iron-on adhesive webs (Bondaweb, Wonderunder etc)

If you have never used an iron-on adhesive, here are a few tips. There are several brands, and most work in a similar way.

- First, cover your ironing area with baking parchment or greaseproof paper. With the paper backing still in place put the sheet or cut area of iron-on adhesive onto the back of your fabric. Iron over the paper and the protective layer, working the iron slowly and steadily across the whole area. Be methodical so that you don't miss bits. (Note that if you're tracing a design onto your bonding web, it's easier to do the tracing before you iron the web onto your fabric.)

- Turn over to the right side of the fabric and check that you don't have any nips or bubbles; smooth with the iron on the fabric surface. Leave to cool. Never try to remove the backing paper until it's cool, as the adhesive tends to lift with the paper if you do. Draw the shapes you need to cut out on to the paper backing: **remember** that you will need to trace or draw the image you want in reverse, as you are drawing it on the back of your fabric.

- Cut out the shape, remove the paper backing, and position the cutout in the correct place on the front of your quilt. When you are sure you have everything in the right place, cover with greaseproof paper and iron into position. Now you are ready to hand or machine stitch around the edge of the shape.

Where to see Quilts in Scotland

Shows

- Scotland's largest quilt show is the annual Loch Lomond Quilt Show, held in May between Dumbarton and Loch Lomond.
www.lochlomondquiltshow.com

- Grosvenor Exhibitions Ltd also hold events near Edinburgh twice a year.
www.grosvenorexhibitions.co.uk

The Quilters' Guild

- Region 16 (Scotland) of the Quilters' Guild of the British Isles holds two Regional days each year, and smaller area days in between. You don't have to be a member to go – but it's cheaper if you are! Information and contact details are on their website.
www.quiltersguild.org.uk

Local Guilds

- Many local patchwork and quilting groups put on their own shows. The guilds also often have talks by visiting quilters, hire collections for an evening, or show work by their own members. Look in local papers and patchwork and quilting magazines, and search the internet.

Scottish Textile Heritage

www.scottishtextileheritage.org.uk

Museums

- **Burrell Collection, Glasgow**
The Burrell has a collection of quilts, quilted items and great textiles, but these are not on permanent display. Contact the Burrell via www.glasgowmuseums.com

- **National Museum, Edinburgh**
The National Museum does have quilts, but not on display. Background to textile industries, Harris Tweed, Turkey Red etc.
www.nms.ac.uk

- **National Museum of Costume, Dumfries**
One or two quilts, but great generally for textile lovers.
www.nms.ac.uk

- **You can also search under:**
www.museumsgalleriesscotland.org.uk, for smaller local museums and galleries.

- Look for museums in areas with textile connections, such as Clydebank Museum, with connections to the Singer factory and to the Turkey Red industry. Paisley Museum has connections to Paisley shawls, Coats threads etc; Hawick Museum has connections to knitting.

Art Schools

- Glasgow School of Art, Glasgow, and Duncan of Jordanstone College of Art and Design in Dundee, both house part of the National Needle Development Collection of Textiles.

- Collins Gallery, University of Strathclyde, Glasgow often have textile-themed exhibitions including Quilt Art and similar groups.
www.strath.ac.uk/collinsgallery/

Thanks and References

With Thanks

Homecoming Scotland

Janet Rae

All supporters of the Loch Lomond Quilt Show

Makepeace Quilters

Students of the Studio

The Quilters of Scotland

Churches of Dumbarton and the Vale of Leven

West Dunbartonshire Council, Arts Development Team, Library and Archive services

Photographs by

Steven Woodward

Ruth Higham

Gordon Hurrell: *The Tartan Holdall Collection*

Iain Wilson at Photo Ecosse (Dumbarton): *Back cover and page 2*

Patricia Macindoe

www.bigstockphoto.com: *page 46*

References

Making Connections by Janet Rae and Dinah Travis

Quilt Treasures – The Quilters' Guild of the British Isles

Seeing Red by Liz Arthur

The Quilts of the British Isles by Janet Rae

Quilted Planet by Celia Eddy

Traditional British Quilts by Dorothy Osler